released

By

Megan Duncan

All rights reserved.
Copyright © 2011 by Megan Duncan

Second Edition: March 2011

This is a work of fiction. Any resemblance of characters to actual persons, living or dead, is purely coincidental. The author holds exclusive rights to this work. Unauthorized duplication is prohibited.

For information:
http://meganduncan.blogspot.com/

Released

ISBN-13: 978-1461017721
ISBN-10: 1461017726

For my husband - Without you none of this would have been possible.

Chapter 1

I am sitting in my room organizing my duffle bag. Carter, my older brother, said we are leaving tomorrow. It has been six weeks since the last transmission. The last news we heard was that people were holding up at a military base in New Mexico. When we stopped hearing anything, Carter got it in his head to go there and help in the fight.

Now I'm trying to decide which belongings I can take and what has to be left behind.

"You gonna be ready by morning Abby?" Carter asked. I simply stared at my newly painted nails, which I had already started to pick at. At least I had picked the right color, black suited my mood perfectly.

"Still sulking I see." Max, my brother's best friend, taunted me as he walked past my room. So, I gave him the single digit salute and he just laughed as he continued on down the hall.

"Listen Abby, we're going to be fine. Max and I have a plan. You know I would never let anything hurt you right?"

"I know," I said defeated. That was Carter, always trying to be my guardian. His heart was in the right place, but I knew in the end it would be me protecting him.

"Besides..." he added. "Don't you want to have the chance to get revenge for Dad?" He had me there.

"You know I do," I said as he mussed my hair and left the room. Our dad died four months ago trying to save our neighbor from one of those damn monsters.

Just got the both of them killed in the end, whole lot of good that did. There was one thing the three of us did agree on though, and that was that we wanted to kill every last one of those things.

No one knew what to make of it at first. People started mysteriously going missing, only to turn back up mutilated by some animal that nobody could determine. It wasn't until they started showing themselves that all hell broke loose.

Crime went rampant without punishment. It came to a point where it was hard to tell if it was the monsters committing the heinous acts or people. However, there were many who turned to religion, shouting in the streets to repent your sins, claiming that God was punishing us. I for one, wasn't sure I believed that.

Carter paid close attention to all the different attacks while the media was still working, cataloging all the information. The best way to beat them he'd say, "You got to know what you're fighting Abby." He sounded just like our dad when he said that. Our father had started the book and it appeared to be Carter's intention to finish it.

So far we had only encountered two types. The hound, which I thought looked like some kind of cross between a Rottweiler and a bull, was the first type we encountered. It had pitch black fur, black horns and it stunk of rotting meat. It was easy to know they were nearby due to the smell, but impossible to find if it was dark.

The other was some kind of bird that looked like a crow bred with a vulture. They were large, ominous beasts with beady black eyes and a razor sharp beak. Max and I would bicker about what we should call them. I wanted to call them crowtures even though I knew it sounded terrible and Max wanted to call them cravens. Eventually we agreed to disagree and Carter deemed them demon birds.

It was fitting. That is what they are. The world was being overrun with demon spawn. Hell was overflowing and heaven had checked out. All that was left were us humans trying to survive and clean up the mess.

After I finished packing, I found Carter in the

dining room making notes in his demon dictionary. In it, we would write tips of what we found worked and what didn't. Drawings of what they looked like and their behaviors, but we didn't see much in our little town, so that book wasn't very big. As far as we could tell, the hounds were territorial, fighting primarily in groups no larger than two. The demon birds, however, were very much like scavengers and only looked for the remains of what the hounds left behind. We had never seen or heard of any attack by the birds, but whenever we saw one flying circles in the sky we knew they had found someone dead, or worse someone dying.

"You gonna stare at me all night?" Carter asked.

I slid into the chair across from him and started to clean my shotgun. I set my cleaning kit on the table and began to unscrew the nut to remove the barrel.

"Carter, do you really think Dad would want us to leave?" I asked as I set the disconnected barrel on the table and grabbed my bore rod. I saw Carter roll his eyes at me and I knew he wanted to tell me that my gun didn't need cleaning, but I did it when I was worried. It was the last thing my father taught me how to do and I suppose, like him, I needed something that reminded me of my Dad to hold onto.

"Yeah I do Abby. If we are able to help people, he would want us to do that," he said as he scratched his head.

"I made dinner." Max proclaimed somewhat proudly as he pulled up a chair.

I eyed his bowl of beans and my stomach turned. "Thanks," I said. "So what's the plan boys?"

"I thought you said we were crazy," Max replied.

"I did and you are, but someone has to watch out for you," I said. Max smiled at me and went back to eating.

"Well…" Carter said while setting down his pencil. "It's simple. We are packing up the Bronco in the morning, we are heading to New Mexico *and*" he added with strong annunciation, "we are going to kill every demon we see along the way."

"Alright then," I said. It was still a crazy idea, but he was all the family I had left and I wasn't going to let him out of my sight. "So how do you plan to get us there Carter? That is like two thousand miles away right?"

"No, it's only fifteen hundred," he said.

"Oh well, if it's only that much," I said sarcastically throwing my hands up in the air.

"Listen Abby, we can't stay here and you know it. We're like sitting ducks," Max said. "Carter is right, we have to go. Eventually we are going to run out of food *and* bullets. What then, huh?"

I looked into his brown eyes and I knew he was right. "Okay," I grumbled and then I reassembled my shotgun in silence and headed to my room.

I had a routine every night before I could go to sleep. I had to check every board over every door and window in the house before I could rest. Sometimes I would even get up during the night to double check. I had scared Max really bad once, when he had first come to stay with us. He'd shot me, but luckily it was only a flesh wound on my right arm. Good thing he was a bad shot. He was still so jumpy after losing his family, I was actually apologizing to him even though I was the one who got hurt.

"Good to go Abby?" he asked every night now

before he would lie down to sleep.

"Yep," I replied as I zipped up my duffel bag and sat on my bed. He began to walk away, but popped his head back in, "Good night Abby."

"Good night Max," I replied with a smile. He looked at me for a moment and a small smile spread across his lips.

"I see you still got that ratty old bear I gave you," Max said.

"Yep," I said as I looked down at my one-eyed, one-legged teddy bear. It had gone through many teenage hormone filled tantrums and many tug of war fights with Carter's dog and me dripping with tears.

"How old were you then?" Max asked as he leaned up against my desk.

"Thirteen. I got in that fight with a girl at school and you let me have him, so I would stop crying," I said laughing through the memory.

"What's so funny?"

"Do you remember what happened the next day?" I asked. "I got suspended for beating that girl up during lunch in the cafeteria."

Max laughed out loud. "Yeah! You gave her a nasty black eye and a bloody nose too. I remember when they asked you why you did it. You said..."

"I'm not going to let anyone think they can beat me," we said in unison.

"You always were a sore loser," he said with a wry smile and flicked a paper clip at me as he walked out of my room.

After my mother died I always tried to be the tough girl. I wanted everyone to know that I wasn't afraid of anyone or anything, but when I discovered that I had been successful I realized that I had convinced everyone of that except for myself.

I used to be excited to wake up early the morning of a road trip, but not this time. I dragged myself out of bed when I could hear the sounds of Carter and Max moving about the house. I quickly turned on the radio on my dresser hoping to hear something other than static, but there was nothing. I just needed to hear something, just some small bit of the transmission that had repeated so many times in the past. I turned the knob through all the dials and angrily slammed the off button.

Looking at myself in the mirror I tried to recognize this new person I was becoming. I looked older and tired, but I tried to convince myself it was just because of a lack of sleep. I traded in my flip flops for my favorite pair of converse sneakers. Straying away from my typical short and tank-top attire I pulled on some jeans and a t-shirt. Gone were the days of sunbathing and shopping with my friends.

I had put on my favorite high school shirt, which brought back memories of football games and shouting, "Go Indians!" at the top of my lungs. It was sad to think just six months ago I was worried about who to go to prom with and now I was worried about staying alive.

I tied my rebellious brown hair up into a messy bun and tried to mentally prepare myself for the road ahead.

"Looking good Abby, you ready to go?"

"As ready as I'll ever be." I thought for a second and said, "Hey Max!"

"Yeah?"

"If we are going to do this, you got to promise

me one thing." He grabbed my bag for me as we made our way down the stairs.

"You got it." His answer was a little too quick for my liking.

"Max I'm serious." I watched him drop my bag by the front door. He turned and looked at me with his arms crossed over his chest.

When I knew I was getting his full attention I said, "Promise me you'll look out for Carter." I looked in his eyes pleading. He walked over to me and put his arm over my shoulder.

"Listen Abs." I hate it when he calls me that. "I won't let anything happen to either of you. You're all I got left." He gave me a hug and whispered, "I promise" in my ear before releasing me to find Carter.

Being outside was very eerie. It was disturbingly quiet and any tiny sound we made seemed to be amplified. After loading up the Bronco we all climbed in and said goodbye to the only home we had ever known.

Max drove while Carter scribbled away in his book. I broke the silence first. "I had almost forgot it was nearly Christmas when everything happened."

We passed by houses with lights still hung and deflated yard ornaments smeared with blood. I wasn't sure if I liked the fact that there weren't any bodies. No bodies meant they had been dragged off or eaten.

Going down main street was an even sadder sight. Store fronts were littered with broken glass; cars were crashed into each other or in buildings and some of the trees that lined the street were blackened from fire.

We made our way off of the dirt roads and toward the central drag of our little town of Colville, WA. We decided to stay on Main Street until it turned into Highway 395 and headed south, slowly weaving our way through the wreckage. Again no bodies. All that remained was blood, entrails and the occasional left over limb.

"Do you think we should stop for extra supplies?" I asked. "A small town like ours is more likely to have stuff left then any big city we might pass through."

"She has a point," Max added, and we both looked to Carter.

"Yep, you're probably right," he said without even looking up. Max and I both rolled our eyes and decided to stop at the Yoke's grocery store about fifty miles south of us. Neither of us wanted to go to a store we knew well, on the off chance we might see someone we knew, or more like a piece of someone we knew.

"What are you writing in there anyway Carter? Don't you think it would benefit us if we all knew?" I hadn't meant to snap at him, but I was still on edge about this trip and he was my easiest target at the moment.

"There aren't any bodies; I just thought that is kind of weird. That's all." Carter turned in his seat to look back at me, his blue eyes were full of questions. "What do you think?" he asked.

"Yeah, I was thinking the same thing. Do you think they're eating them?" A shiver rolled down my spine as I said it.

"Or maybe everyone else got away and they just didn't tell us," Max added with a crooked smile while looking at me through the rear view mirror.

"Shut up Max," I replied, making sure my tone wasn't too harsh.

"What? I was just trying to lighten the mood." We tried making small talk for the next few miles, but it felt forced, so we all sat in silence until we arrived at the market an hour later. It was still too early in our journey to know for sure, whether or not this was a good idea.

Chapter 2

A mountain of shopping carts were stacked haphazardly near the main entrance. We had each opted for quieter weapons, as to not draw unwanted attention, but I always kept my shotgun on me. Max had grabbed one of our old wood chopping axes, which I had voted we not bring because it was dull and there was no way to sharpen it plus the blade head was coming loose from the handle. I obviously lost that argument but we did all have large hunting knives strapped to our legs.

A few days ago Max had gone to our local fish and game store to salvage what he could. He had managed the knives, some handguns and a crossbow for Carter. He wasn't as good at hand to hand as Max and I, but he was a very good shot. Which he attributes to all the hours of HALO he use to play. I rolled my eyes at that comment, but I couldn't argue with him, he was a good shot.

I had emptied my duffel bag into the back of the Bronco before we started to head in. Moving the carts was out of the question so we opted to push a nearby car under a broken window at a side entrance to the right.

"Carter you stay by the window and watch our backs." He already had an arrow loaded and the strap for his knife was undone.

"Got it. You two make it quick and stay together."

Max grabbed the empty duffel bag and swung it over his shoulder as we made our way between the registers. We both quickly turned at the sound of DVD cases falling to the tile floor.

"Sorry." Carter whispered and Max and I just

mumbled under our breath and continued walking. We headed straight for the middle of the store, avoiding the perishable food lining the outer aisles that had rotted long ago.

"You think he's ok by himself?" Max asked as we reached the canned goods.

"I'd rather have him there, then in here. It's safer. At least he can make a run for the Bronco if he needs to." Max nodded silently. We both had an unspoken understanding that we felt Carter was the most valuable of the three of us. He was the brains behind our little operation, and if we were ever going to survive this, it would be because of Carter.

I watched Max as he removed the bag from off his back. "Keep an eye out while I fill this," I told him as I took the bag from his grasp. Our fingers brushed slightly and I did my best to act as if I didn't notice. I dropped the bag and opened it, surveying the shelves of what was available.

Max walked further down the aisle to scout more of the store while I grabbed what food I could, staying away from anything with blood on it. Seeing him standing guard over me made a flush of warmth flow through me, but I pushed it away. There were more important things I needed to focus on at the moment.

We quietly made our way through more aisles, picking up what we could, until we found ourselves standing before the double doors to the back of the store.

"What do you think?" I asked Max.

"I think you're crazy, but maybe we could find something useful back there I guess. It's risky though." He whipped the sweat from his brow with the back of his hand. "It's your call Abs."

"Let's go," I said as I zipped up the bag and handed it to him. I took the lead since I was unencumbered and pushed open the doors.

I was preparing myself for a demon, but the smell of decomposing bodies is what almost overpowered me. I fought back the urge to vomit as I pulled a rag from out of my pocket and held it over my nose and mouth. I looked back to Max for his reaction.

"Damn! There are bodies here," he looked as shocked as I did, as he surveyed the room.

From what we could tell it seemed like a group

of people were trying to hold out here. There were a few cots and chains on the outer doors. Body parts lay strewn all over, mostly in the small sleeping area they had set up.

"Looks like they got them when they were sleeping." Max pointed out to a woman still lying in a cot. Her face was frozen in horror. Long deep gashes were torn across her chest. Another person was completely mauled. The head had been torn clean off and they were rolled over onto their side in a fetal position. They probably didn't even see it coming.

"Poor bastards," Max commented quietly.

Stepping through as quietly as we could, we found the office door. A man's hand hung from the door knob in a frozen death grip. I was afraid I would have to break a couple fingers to get it off, but Max was able to pry it loose. As he went to lay the severed hand down on a cot, the door slowly creaked open and we both froze. A wave of nauseating odor wafted from the room, carrying the smell of rotting meat.

"Go!" Max shouted as he shoved me out the double doors. I glimpsed a flash of silver as I fell to the ground. I got up to pull my gun free as the hound came barreling out the doors toward me. Max's knife was buried to the hilt, deep into its side and it didn't seem to slow it in the least.

It swung at me and missed, but got me on the back swing taking my feet out from under me. It sent me tumbling into a shelf sending cans of dog food down on top of me. My shotgun had been knocked free and was too far out of my reach.

The hound lunged to bite at my leg sending bloody drool flying, but I pulled away and kicked it hard in the head. I dazed it only for a second and it lunged at me again.

I grabbed a can of food and chucked it at its grotesque face as hard as I could, and then another. I dove for my shotgun and my fingers closed around the cool smooth metal.

As I rolled over cocking it, the hound was charging for me. It let out a deep guttural growl as bloody slobber dripped from its mouth.

I aimed and shoved the barrel of the gun in its mouth and pulled the trigger as it bit at me. The hounds head exploded, sending blood and brain matter everywhere. The dead weight of its body fell onto me and pinned me to the ground. Hot blood poured onto my chest and neck as it seeped out of the open wound in a sudden rush.

"Abby!" Carter shouted as he came running down the aisle.

"Get this demon off me!" I grunted as I pushed.

"Are you ok? What happened? Where's Max?" Carter hammered me with questions.

"Shit Max!" I shouted as we rolled the beast off me. "Carter get Max's knife." I ordered as I ran for the double doors.

"I got it!" Carter called out as he followed after me. I heard the squeak of his boots as he stepped through the puddle of blood on the tile floor leaving bloody footprints in his wake.

I found Max slumped on the ground near a far wall and ran for him. Carter stayed by the door and when I heard him vomiting I ordered for him to suck it up and help me. As we lifted Max up to a sitting position, I took the bag from off of his back.

"Did I get him?" Max asked wearily. A smile crept on my face as I sighed in relief.

"Yeah," I lied. "You got 'em. Are you hurt Max?"

He began a pat down of himself and located a gash on his leg. "We will get that fixed up in the Bronco," I said.

"He charged at me and slammed me into the wall. I remember shoving my knife into its body, then...then... I must have blacked out."

"You're lucky you didn't get eaten!" Carter said harshly holding up the broken axe like some kind of evidence. "What the hell were you doing or what the hell weren't you doing? You almost got Abby killed!"

"What?" Max looked at me and his eyes grew wide at the sight of me covered in blood.

"Shut it Carter! It wasn't Max's fault, he shoved me out of the way, but..." then I realized, "it didn't go after him. It knocked you out of the way." I pointed to Max, "And then it ran out through the doors and saw me."

"So..." Carter said with a bit of attitude.

"I don't think that it liked being locked up," I said. "It wanted out more than it wanted to kill Max."

"Well lucky him. Now come on, we got to get the hell out of here," Carter said as he grabbed the duffel bag and headed out the double doors.

"Can you walk?" I asked Max and he nodded. I took his hands and balanced our weight while he stood himself up.

"Abby," he said as he grabbed my shoulders "I'm sorry. I'm really sorry. I just keep screwing things up." He took the rag from out of my hand and started to wipe the blood off my neck.

"It's ok Max. I'm ok and you're ok." I took the rag back from him and slid my body under his arm and we made our way out of the store as fast as we could.

Max cursed as we walked past the hound. "They smell worse dead then they do alive don't they?" Carter asked.

I could tell his anger had already dissipated and his mind was reeling with the new information we had just discovered. Although I couldn't understand how that knowledge would be of any use to us. So, the hounds didn't like being locked up, big deal. I sure as shit wasn't going to ever try to lock one up myself.

Seeing the blue Bronco parked out front gave me a small burst of adrenaline and I ran for it. Carter already had the engine running by the time Max and I had even opened the back door. I tossed the bag in and we jumped in as Carter sped off. I could have sworn I heard the call of one of those demon birds as we drove away, but I didn't say anything.

I crawled into the back of the Bronco and started digging through our things, looking for our first aid kit.

"Carter, where did you pack the first aid kit?" I asked.

"It's in the green bag. Dad's old A1 bag."

I knew that bag well and found it quickly. I crawled into the seat with Max and tried to assess his wound. He clenched his teeth as I slowly began to pull away his pants from the wound. Pieces of fiber were already sticking.

"Take off your pants," I ordered. Carter must have seen a smile pass Max's face because the Bronco suddenly jerked to the right. I shouted at Carter to watch it and he apologized while constantly looking back at us through the rear view mirror.

As I helped pull his pant legs down, being careful not hit the wound, I was relieved to see the cuts weren't as deep as I had thought. I pulled out what tools I needed from our kit and got to work.

"Ok Max, this is going to hurt. A lot." I looked in his eyes and held up a bottle of alcohol to show him.

"Aren't you supposed to lie to me?"

I smiled. "Oh yes, ok Max, this isn't going to hurt a bit. You're just going to feel a slight tingling sensation and then you'll be right as rain," I said in my best doctoral tone.

He started to laugh, so I poured a bit of the alcohol on his wound and he yelled out in agony. The wounds bubbled up and I quickly placed a piece of gauze over it pressing down as hard as I could.

Max pressed his head back and closed his eyes letting out a moan as I slowly pried the gauze off and placed a couple bandages over the wound trying to close it up the best I could. After placing another piece of gauze on it and securing the bandage, I assured Max I wouldn't have to take the leg and he laughed.

Feeling the blood starting to dry on my skin, I quickly wanted to clean myself up. Small chunks of demon hound were stuck in my hair and I tried to control the bile rising up my throat while I pulled them out.

I crawled into the back again and took off my t-shirt. I rolled it into a ball and shoved into a side pocket of my duffel bag, I wanted to try to clean it someday, if I could. After a thorough wipe down using baby wipes we swiped from the store, I pulled on a black top with a picture of Eeyore and the words *Moody* on the front. I let Max take the back seat so he could keep his leg straight as I crawled up front with Carter and grabbed our map.

"So where are we?" I asked.

"We are about ten minutes outside of Spokane I think."

"Wow already?" I said. "I didn't think we would hit a bigger city so quickly. What's the plan?"

"I think we should just stay on the highway and try to make it through as quickly and quietly as possible. Keep an eye on the map for me though Abby, just in case we have to make a detour."

"So what are you thinking Carter?" I asked.

"What?"

"Come on," I said. "I can almost hear the wheels spinning up there," and I tapped him on the head.

"Geez Abby," he said as he took the folded up map and slapped me on the leg with it. "Grab my book from the glove box would ya? Open it to the fifth page."

I turned the pages and found Carter's almost illegible handwriting describing the hounds. I wrote down what Carter told me to after I had narrated what happened at the back of the store. He seemed to relax a bit after we had added the information to the book, I'm sure he would read through it a million times as soon as he got the chance.

I wanted to tease him every time I saw him with it, but I was starting to understand his need for it. This book was his lifeline to reality, or at least the reality that we once knew. It was *his* ticket to our old way of life, and whether or not it would really be of any help in the end didn't matter right now. What really mattered was that it was getting him through each day.

It had taken much longer to get through town. We would occasionally get out, to move a car out of the way and other times we would have to take side streets, which we wanted to avoid as much as possible. There were too many places for things to hide.

As we neared the center of town, the tall brick buildings loomed over us. I got the feeling that something was watching us, but no matter how many dark windows I looked into I couldn't find anything. Crossing over the Spokane River, I saw that a car had gone over the side of the bridge. I tried to look down into the car as we drove by but it was too hard to see.

"Where are we?" Max asked from the backseat.

"Spokane, but once we get through here and Coeur D'Alene it should be an easier drive for a bit. Hopefully," I said. "You feeling better?"

"Yeah thanks. Damn, this place looks like a war zone." He commented while looking out the window.

"Shit, the entrance to the interstate is blocked off," Carter said as we approached I-90. A huge semi had flipped onto its side across the entrance.

"I'm sure we can find another ramp to go up," I

said as I pointed to my left. "Looks like that road follows along the interstate, let's take that until we can get on."

Carter put the Bronco in gear and we started our way down Mission Avenue. Max and I pointed out things along the way. Vandals had written eerie sayings on buildings, announcing that the end of the world was near or that the devil had come to earth. I didn't want to think that they were probably right.

After a good number of blocks we found an entrance and made our way onto the interstate.

"Wow, look at all the smoke," Max said and we all looked. Towers of black smoke rose up throughout the whole city.

"Max look over here," I said as I tapped my finger on the window. He scooted over to the right side of the car and looked out the window.

"What am I looking for?" he asked.

"Just above the tree tops," I said. "There are birds."

"Crap." Carter let out an aggravated groan and stopped the Bronco.

"What?" Max and I both turned in unison and saw what Carter was looking at. The whole road was barricaded with cars.

"How are we going to get through that?" I asked.

"We are going to have to back track, go back on the surface streets until we can find an entrance past this," Carter said.

"That doesn't sound like a good idea," I said. I punched the dash and stepped out of the car, shutting the door as quietly as I could.

"What the hell Abby!" Carter tried his hardest to yell at me and whisper at the same time. He ran his fingers through his greasy blonde hair and headed toward me. "What do you want me to do, huh?"

I looked at the Bronco and saw Max sitting up, staring through the windshield at me, giving me his best what the hell are you doing look.

"I just don't want to go back on the streets Carter, I have a bad feeling. Can't we just move these cars like we did the other ones?" I asked.

"There are too many Abby," he said with his voice full of annoyance.

"No... we just need to make enough room for the Bronco, we don't have to move them all." I waved my arm toward the pile of wreckage in a Vanna White type motion and started walking toward the smallest car I could see, a bright yellow beetle near the shoulder. I peered inside and saw the keys were still in the ignition.

"Well?" Carter asked creeping up behind me with his fists resting on his hips, looking very much like how I thought out mother looked.

"The keys are in the ignition, if we can move this beetle and maybe that truck we can squeeze through, what do you think?"

He eyed the space I was proposing and then looked back at the Bronco and then back again. "Maybe... but we got to do this quick Abby. I think we are going to have to move the cars at the same time while Max drives the Bronco through. I'm guessing we have one shot at this," he said as he jerked his head toward the hill I had seen the birds. "Before *they* notice."

Chapter 3

I knew Max was up for my idea before we even told him. It took some time to get him into the front seat and I had to move his injured leg for him and place it on the clutch. Max placed his hand on Carter's shoulder and I let them have some space, while I'm sure Max was vowing not to screw anything up and Carter was being overly technical trying to tell Max what he needed to do.

Looking at the two of them you would never guess the two were best friends. Carter was six foot, super slender and a geek to his core while Max was the tall, dark and brooding type. The captain of our high school's football team and until everything happened he was on track to join the marines. When they were young, Carter saved Max from drowning at the public pool and they have been inseparable ever since.

Carter and I crawled into the cars and we gave each other a final glance before we started the engines. He was going to have to move the truck first before I could move because the front end of the beetle was wedged underneath the bed of the truck. As Carter started to pull away he dragged me with him making a loud scrapping sound as the weak metal of the beetle scrapped against the pavement. He looked back at me, a flash of panic playing on his face and I saw him try to peer over at the birds on the hill.

Then we heard their low shrieks as the four birds formed together and shot down the hillside toward us. I put the beetle in gear and slammed my foot on the gas trying to pry myself free of the truck. My wheels spun sending white smoke flying behind me and the smell of burning rubber into the air. We were stuck and I was starting to worry, knowing this was my bad idea.

I looked over to the Bronco, wondering if I should make a run for it when I saw Max signaling Carter. Max was hurtling toward us and aimed the Bronco for the side of the truck. I braced myself for the impact as it came crashing into me.

Max then drove the Bronco into reverse and Carter took off in the truck squealing its tires. I shook off the shock of what had happened and moved the smashed up beetle as fast as it would go. I jumped out and ran for the Bronco as fast as I could. I heard Carter yell my name and I looked at him as he pointed a handgun at me.

"Down!" he shouted.

I dropped to the pavement, scraping up my arms as I tried to break the fall and heard Carter let out four bullets, followed by the loud shriek of a demon bird and an explosion of black feathers. The beating of their huge wings was terrifying and I felt strong arms grab me by my shoulders and pull me up toward the back of the

Bronco.

"You ok?" Carter asked giving me a quick look over then shooting back at a bird that dove at us. "Get in the car!" he shouted.

I crawled in through the back window and grabbed my shotgun as Carter jumped in the front seat. Max took off through the gap as fast as he could, clipping the side view mirror on another car, but we made it. Three of the birds followed after us and I shot at them through the back window. After a few miles they gave up their pursuit.

"Holy crap!" Max cheered once we were sure they had gone. "That was damn close."

"Too close," I said. "We should probably stop soon Max and get you out of that driver's seat. You need to rest up that leg."

"I'm fine," he said as he waved me off.

"Next time will you go with my idea Abby?" Carter asked as he turned around to face me.

"Hopefully there won't be a next time," I said.

We decided that we would wait until after the next city to pull over for a break. Making it through the rest of the city was quicker than we had thought as the roads were more open, but the tall pine trees lining the roads seemed to tower eerily over us.

It was afternoon now, but the sky was overcast and a light drizzle of rain started to fall. As we drove along lake Coeur D'Alene I watched a fog roll in and silently prayed that the rest of the journey would go more smoothly. About twenty miles outside of Missoula we pulled off the road to go to the bathroom. I was still shook up from earlier, so I wasn't too fond of the idea of going very far into the woods to pee, so I found a nearby tree not caring about privacy at the moment.

Walking back up the embankment I saw Max leaning against the front of the Bronco. He had changed into a clean flannel shirt and was cleaning his fingers nails with the tip of his knife. I looked at him for a moment before approaching him, admiring how handsome he was.

"How's the leg?" I asked as I rested my back on the front of the Bronco beside him.

"Fine. You hungry?"

"Starving." I hadn't realized it until he had asked.

"Let me see what we got."

I walked over to the back of the Bronco and found some canned peaches and beef jerky. With three cans and a bag of jerky in hand I walked back up to Max and deposited the items on the hood.

Max opened a can for me and one for himself and we both ate in silence until Carter joined us.

"So I was thinking, there is a summer camp not far from here, we should hold up for the night there," Carter said while wiping peach syrup from his chin.

"You don't think we should try to drive through the night?" I asked yanking a big chunk of jerky off with my teeth and handing it to Max.

"Yeah, I thought that was the plan," Max added.

"It was, but after all the action" - he made air quotations with his fingers at that word – "we've seen today, I think it might do us some good to lay low for a little while," Carter said.

Max and I looked at each other and he shrugged his shoulders.

"Look," Carter said as he pulled the map from his back pocket. He unfolded it and held it out for us to see, showing us where we were and where the camp was. Or where he thought it was.

"Carter what if it is not even there?" Max asked.

"It is! Trust me. I was suppose to go there my sophomore year and be a camp counselor, but I failed shop class so my dad wouldn't let me."

I held back a snicker and said, "Yeah, Mr. Brooks was a real jerk. He didn't like you much."

"I would have had straight A's that year if it weren't for him, but that doesn't matter now. How are we on gas?"

"Um…" I said as I ran back to the Bronco and turned the key, "a little more than a quarter tank."

"Ok, that should get us there, but we are going to have to get gas soon. You grabbed the hose, right Max?"

"Yeah, but if we are going to be siphoning gas often, I say we take turns," Max said as he tossed his empty can of peaches into the brush.

"Fine with me," I said as I hoped into the driver's seat.

"You say that now, but you have no idea how

terrible gasoline tastes," Max replied.

We drove on quietly, as a light summer rain pelted the Bronco. I was starting to think this whole thing was a bad idea, and I was sure everyone else was too. What were we thinking? I was a magnet for trouble and Carter was all brains and no brawns, but Max, he could make it I thought. He was tough and strong, but I knew the responsibility of taking care of Carter and me, must be weighting on him.

I stole glances at him as I drove down the highway. He sat silently, surveying the landscape making comments about a particular wrecked vehicle or the amount of garbage that littered the streets. I never said anything, feeling that the comments were more of him just thinking aloud to distract himself from what was really on his mind.

Carter sprawled out in the back seat, well, as much as a six foot person could sprawl out in a back seat. He had read through his book multiple times, asking for our opinion occasionally but was now drifting off to sleep with the book resting tightly in his grasp.

"Do you really think there are people still in New

Mexico?" I blurted out to Max without even thinking.

After a long pause he said, "I have to Abs, if we can't believe in that then what are we even doing?"

"It's hard for me to believe in anything anymore," I said as I gripped the steering wheel until my knuckles turned white.

"Listen Abby, you are too hard on yourself. I think you are a lot tougher then you realize. You were raised by two men, a retired marine and your big brother. You're a tough cookie *and* a bit of a tomboy," he said.

"Yeah, yeah, I know." I hated being reminded of it. Being a tomboy was always the kiss of death in my relationships. It was comforting to know that Max thought I was tough, but little did he realize that it was all a charade because I was too afraid to let anyone know how sensitive I really was.

"I don't know how you were friends with that Heather girl, she was a little Princess, that one," he said scornfully.

"Me? You dated her Max," I said playfully.

"Yeah, well only for like three weeks and besides she tricked me, I didn't really like her to begin with."

"How does someone trick you into dating them? Did she tell you she knew the secret to winning the state championship or something?" I smiled at him.

"Something like that, yeah," he said.

I watched him scratch at his growing beard and wondered what would have been.

"What are you thinking?" he asked.

"What makes you think I am thinking something?"

"You are always thinking something Abs," he said.

"I was thinking about Prom," I said, eyeing him, waiting for him to start laughing.

"What?"

"No witty reply to that one?" I was actually quite shocked. All my life Max had teased me every chance he got and now in the middle of a demon apocalypse, I was thinking about the Prom and he had nothing to say about it.

"Ya know Abs…" he said slowly, "I was actually thinking I was going to ask you to Prom."

My heart started pounding in my chest and I

realized I hadn't said anything when I heard Max say, "Hello Abby, anybody home?"

"Sorry."

"So that bad, eh? Next time a guy tells you he wanted to ask you out, you might want to let him down a little easier," he said almost amused.

"No... I... uh.." I started stuttering not knowing what to say. I wanted to tell him how I felt, that I thought he was the hottest thing on earth but when it came to men, at least sexy men, I was a total wimp.

Max started to laugh and when he looked ahead his face fell. "Abby stop the car!" he shouted. "Stop the car, stop the car!" he repeated quickly.

"What?" As I said it I saw what he was seeing and I slammed on the brakes. Just around a bend in the road about a hundred yards ahead of us, a minivan was flipped over, but that wasn't the worst part. Three birds were pecking at a body on the street and they just drew their attention toward us.

"What should we do?" I asked as I watched one of the birds jump to the top of the van to get a better view of us.

"I don't know. Carter, wake up man. Wake up!"

Carter bolted awake in a sudden flourish. He was about to start shouting, but I clamped my hand down on his mouth and pointed out the windshield. When he nodded his recognition I released my hand.

"What do you think we should do?" I asked Carter.

"Maybe we should just drive through them?" Max offered. "I mean we can't exactly go back."

I turned around in the driver's seat and watched the birds as Max and Carter tried to figure out what we should do. It seemed to me that at the moment the birds feast was more important, so that bought us some time. As I watched them something caught my eye, a movement. Not made by the birds, but by someone or something inside the van.

"Carter," I said as loudly as I could, but he didn't hear me because he was in a debate with Max about what we should do. Carter wanted to turn back and Max thought we should just put our foot on the gas and barrel through them. I thought that was a damn good idea, but with what I had to say, there might be a change of plans.

"Carter!" I grabbed him on the shoulder and waved my hand in front of his face to get his attention.

"What Abby?" he said annoyed and when he saw my reaction he immediately softened.

"Tell me what you see inside that van."

Carter leaned over the front seat and rested his hands on the dashboard. He squinted hard and I silently watched him as a drop of sweat rolled down his temple.

"Holy shit," he said as his mouth dropped.

"What?" Max asked. "What do you see?"

"There is someone inside of that van," I said. When his face still looked confused I added, "alive." Max's eyes opened wide and he quickly pushed Carter aside to have a look for himself.

"Well we gotta get them," Max said.

That being his first reaction, made my feelings for him grow. He was so much like my father. Everything I respected in a man; brave, honorable and selfless. He always wanted to play the hero no matter what the risk.

"What are you crazy?" Carter said. "That might not even be a person, it could be a demon bird inside that van, or it could be something else. You really want to take that risk?"

"Carter, you said yourself that the whole point of this trip was to kill every damn demon we saw, well I see three right there!" Max said pointing his finger out the windshield.

"So do I." I added for good measure.

After a short pause Carter gave in to our reasoning. "You're right," Carter admitted while dropping back into the seat. "What do you think we should do?"

I watched him sit there for a moment, all our minds reeling, trying to figure out what to do. Carter picked at the little crocodile emblem on his polo shirt, while Max rifled through what weapons we had and mumbling about how much ammo was left.

"I think we should stick with Max's idea," I said trying to convey as much confidence as I could even though I was starting to feel the fear creep in. "I say we haul ass to that van and we each unload on a bird. There are three of us and three of them. Sounds pretty damn even to me. If there really is someone inside that van, we take them with us."

Chapter 4

"Sounds good to me," Max said quickly and I smiled at him.

"Carter?" Max asked for confirmation.

"Ok, but we need to plan it out a little better than that. We can't all pick the same target. Abby you drive, stop at about twenty feet away and take out one of the birds on the body and I'll take out the other. Max you ride shotgun. Take out the bird on top of the van and jump out to see if someone is inside. Ok?"

We both nodded and got into our positions. I looked over to Max before starting up the Bronco. "Your leg good to go for this?"

"Hell yes," he said while he pulled down the hammer on his gun. It was bizarre to me how at that moment, my body prickling with fear of what we were about to do that I found Max to be incredibly sexy. Leave it to me to think of something completely off the wall when my attention should be directed to more important matters at hand.

I took a deep breath and focused my thoughts before I put the Bronco in gear and slammed my foot on the gas pedal. As we came speeding down the road the demon birds started shrieking loudly and spreading their wings in an almost challenging posture.

"Now!" Carter shouted as we got near the van.

The Bronco jerked to a stop and I pulled my shotgun from off my lap and fired at the demon bird closest to the Bronco. The bird flew backward landing in a giant feathery heap. I saw one of Carter's arrows land into the other bird with a solid thud.

The one I had shot was struggling to get up and

its eyes locked onto me. I fired again the same time as Max shot at the one on the van and my ears rang from the assault on my ear drums.

Carter opened the back to jump out and retrieve the arrow and I ran to Max as he approached the van with his gun raised. His movements were unwavering and confident, taking the short strides to the passenger side door without hesitation.

As I neared the wrecked van I tried to peer into the windshield to see who or what was inside, but the cracked glass made it impossible to see. The spider web of silver lines completely blocked whatever was inside from view and I wondered how it managed to stay together.

"I'm going to open the door," Max said. I nodded and took a position off to the side, so I could shoot at whatever came out. "We aren't going to hurt you." He spoke toward the van and then I heard him whisper under his breath "unless we have to."

As Max jerked the door open the windshield crumbled into a glittering heap on the dark pavement. I could immediately see the form of a girl sitting with her knees to her chest and her eyes frozen in terror.

"Hey," Max said softly holding out his hand to her. "It's safe now, you can come out."

The girl began to sob uncontrollably and Max got down on his knees to help her out. He nearly dragged her out of the van as she wailed. I thought for a moment that she would start thrashing him, but from the looks of her I was surprised she had the strength to even cry. Her body was frail and dirty and I wondered how long she had been in there.

"My...my mom." She let out in blubbering sobs that were almost unintelligible.

She clung to him weeping, not willing to let go when he tried to pass her to me. He looked to me, confused on what he should do. I stuck my gun into the back of my pants and put my arms around the girl.

My arms felt as if they could wrap around her twice as I held her to me. I tried to think of things to say to comfort her, but all that came to mind were things my Dad would say and I did not think this scrawny, barely teenage girl in my arms could handle it, so I came up with the simplest thing I could.

"It's going to be ok. You're safe now." I didn't really know if that were true or not, but at this point it didn't really matter. She wasn't trapped in that van anymore, so that was an improvement for her.

"We gotta go," Carter said as he came around the back of the Bronco. "Holy shit!" he stopped in his tracks as soon as he spotted the girl in my arms. "It really was a person. What happened?"

"Carter I don't think she can really talk about it right now." I directed his attention toward the body on the ground, but he still wasn't getting it. I then made a mental note to harass my brother about how dense he was.

The girl and I crawled into the back seat and she leaned against the side of the Bronco, silently crying. As Carter hopped into the driver's seat he looked back at us.

"Is she ok?"

"I don't know," I said. He looked at the girl for a moment then started the Bronco. I wasn't quite sure if he was glad we had found someone or not.

As we drove past the van I looked out the window and saw what had made the van flip. A giant hairy mass lay contorted in the road. They must have hit it I thought. I saw Carter look at me in the rear view mirror and I knew he had seen it too. Another terrifying beast to add to his book, but the more we added to it, the more I could tell he was starting to get really scared. We were all starting to get really scared.

After about forty-five minutes, the girl had fallen asleep. I looked down at her and tried to softly pull away the hair that clung to her face, revealing tracks of tears that trailed down her dirty face. She couldn't be much younger than myself, I thought, maybe fourteen or fifteen.

There were cuts and bruises on her arms and I felt an overwhelming urge to protect her. Realizing what she much have gone through, watching her mother get eaten by those demons. I couldn't imagine the horror she must have felt. It made me think of Carter. He was the one that found our father and I knew that the image of that would haunt him the rest of his life. He had saved me from that pain.

It was late one night when we had heard the sounds of our neighbors screaming and my Dad rushed over there to help them. Carter held me back as I chased after my father begging him not to go and begging him to take me with him, to let me help.

But our Dad never came back that night, or that morning. We waited and waited and after two days Carter went next door to find him. I stayed in my room until I heard the sounds of Carter in the backyard and saw the contorted mass wrapped under a blue tarp lying on the ground beside him. We buried our father that day and neither Carter nor I ever went into the backyard again.

The crackling sound of gravel under tires shook me out of my trance and I saw that we had pulled off the road onto a long driveway and passed a large wooden sign that read, "Camp Bug Juice" with the motto "Live, Laugh, Learn" painted underneath and bordered with a rainbow of handprints. It was strange to see something so cheerful after I had visited such a painful memory.

Max and Carter whispered as they tried to decide where we should stay. They had agreed upon a cabin near the camp office labeled the *Eagle's Roost*.

"Abby you two stay here while we take a quick

look around okay?"

"Okay, but be careful Carter. This place is kind of creepy." I looked around and noticed that all the buildings had funny names like *Rabbit Hole* or *Bear Hollow*. It was ironic how a place that would otherwise be full of fun and happiness could look so ominous. It was winter when everything happened, so most likely there was no one here. I tried, but I could not find a drop of blood anywhere. The thought should have comforted me but it didn't.

"Where are we?" the girl asked sitting up.

"Somewhere in Montana, I think, at a summer camp. We are going to stay here for the night," I said trying to sound comforted by that fact. "I'm Abby." I held out my hand to her and smiled.

"Taya," she said as she tugged on the strings of her hoodie and looked down at my open hand but did not take it.

Her eyes shot around wildly, so I put my hand on her knee trying to comfort her. "You're safe now."

She jumped at my touch, recoiling as if I was a monster touching her and I tried not to feel offended.

"There's no such thing as safe. There is alive and there is dead. Anything in between is just dumb luck."

"Well then, I guess we are pretty damn lucky," I said and a tiny smile appeared on her face only to be quickly removed.

"Looks secure," Max said as he popped his head in the driver's window. Taya let out a quick shriek.

"Well hello there, I'm Max," he said with a toothy grin. He opened the door and pushed back the seat so we could exit. Taya was hesitant at first, but took Max's hand when he offered it.

I grabbed my bag before leaving and followed them up the steps into the cabin. It was a lot bigger on the inside then it appeared from outside. There was a small kitchen area to my right, attached to a small dining nook. Two couches faced each other in the living room with a large wooden coffee table in between.

The walls were covered with various artwork, many obviously painted by kids. There were large photographs of groups of people wearing the same colored shirt that I guessed were camp photos of years passed. The children's happy faces smiled back at me and I felt myself grow envious of them, wishing I could feel as happy as they looked.

I saw that Taya had curled up in a chair in a far corner. She held her knees to her chest with one arm and was holding back a curtain with the other, peering out as if she was expecting something to come charging at us at any moment. I figured it was best to leave her be for the moment, so I continued on throughout the cabin.

I tossed my bag on the dining table and made my way to the back of the cabin. There was only one bedroom and one small tiny bathroom, but it was nice enough.

"What do you think Abby?" Carter asked as he walked in carrying a bag he was bringing in from the Bronco.

"It's nice, lots of windows though," I whispered the last part not wanting to worry Taya any more then she already was.

"Yeah, I thought that too. Max went to find the maintenance building to see if he could find some paint."

"Good idea. Have you checked the cabinets yet? Any food?"

"No not yet. So, how is she doing?"

"I'm not sure, she hasn't really said much." We stared at each other for a moment, "I'll try talking to her. See what happened."

"Ok." He patted me on the back and headed for the front door. "I'm going to go find Max and see if I can help him before it starts to get dark."

I looked out the window and noticed the sky was starting to change color, signaling the setting of the sun. I sighed, grateful that the day was over, but this was our first night outside of our house and I wasn't happy about spending the night someplace new.

As I walked toward Taya I tried to think of what I could say to her, then I tried to think of what Carter told me after we lost our father. The girl was obviously scared to death and honestly I was too, even though I tried my hardest not to show it.

I had an idea of something that might help keep her mind off of things, so I turned around and headed into the small kitchen area of the cabin.

"Hey Taya," I called her from the kitchen, but she didn't even flinch, just continued staring through the window.

I continued even though she had ignored me. "You want to help me make us some dinner?"

"Okay," she said and looked out the window one more time before heading for the kitchen. I watched her walk and took notice of how dirty her clothes were. I made a mental note to offer her some clean clothes later. Her black hair hung in knotty, matted ringlets around her face and I could see her boney frame sticking out underneath her clothes. She caught me looking at her and I felt guilty for staring, but I truly did feel sorry for her.

"Alright Taya, why don't you look in the bag over there and see what looks good." When I heard her rummaging through the bag I began to open cabinets looking for anything that might be edible. In the end I found only some rice and a can of expired Campbell's cream of mushroom soup, that I was hoping wouldn't be too far past the expiration date.

"So… Taya, what were you doing out on that road all alone?"

"I wasn't alone. I was with my mom, we were

heading to New Mexico. We had heard over the radio that the military was there, so we were trying to go there."

"What happened?" She froze for a moment while trying to open some canned chicken. I could tell she was struggling on whether or not to tell me. "It looks like you and your mom hit something in the road."

"I don't know what it was, ok? It was d-dark and I was sleeping while my Mom was driving."

"How long were you stuck in that van?"

"Three days."

"I'm sorry Taya. I'm sorry you had to go through that. We are headed to New Mexico too; you are welcome to come with us." I put my arm over her shoulder and tried to comfort her.

"I will take care of you." I meant it too. "How long ago was it that you heard the transmission over the radio?" I tried not to sound too excited about my question. I was growing more and more obsessed with checking the radio as we made our journey, any tiny bit of transmission I could hear would give me the hope I needed. I wanted so badly to know that there were still people at the military base, that there were still people who could help us, who could save us.

"I don't know. It was a while ago." She simply shrugged and didn't look at me. I wanted to ask more questions, but I could tell how difficult it was for her.

We continued with dinner and I tried my best at making casual conversation. Taya told me about her life before. She was a freshman in high school and was excited about making the cheerleading team.

"Your nails are pretty," she commented as we were setting the table.

"Thanks," I said looking down at my bright red fingers. While she was sleeping in the Bronco I dug out my polish and against the protests of Carter and Max, I painted my nails. It was a ridiculous thing to do, but I needed to do something normal to take my mind of reality, anything to keep from thinking that the world was overrun with demons. At the time I had thought red would be a fitting color to represent all the demons we had killed so far. As scary as it was, I was proud that we had managed to kill them, hopefully it meant that, in some way, we had saved someone somewhere from being their victim.

"I have more colors in my bag if you want to try them later." I adjusted the pitch in my voice in an attempt to sound light-hearted, hoping that maybe spending some girl-time with her would help her to feel more comfortable with us.

"That would be cool, but why did you bring them?"

"I don't know. I guess I wanted to have something normal to do, ya know? They don't take much room and I kinda have the habit of painting my nails like once a week. Or at least I use to."

"Cool."

The door then suddenly flew open sending a dead potted plant crashing to the ground causing both Taya and I to jump, nearly spilling dinner all over the dirty linoleum floor. Carter stomped in, his arms filled with wood, followed by Max who was carrying two gallons of paint and tons of sheets.

"Looks like you got what you were looking for," I said smiling at them. I had been worried about them wandering around the camp alone, even if it did look safe to them. Sometimes a guy's standard of what is safe is much different than a woman's, and neither of them were ever described as being very perceptive. Who knows what could be hiding in some vacant cabin.

"Yeah. What smells so good?" Max asked sniffing the hair like a puppy.

"We made dinner," Taya said a little hesitantly, but I could tell she had warmed up to us a bit. I decided to introduce everyone more formally and after a couple handshakes we all sat down to eat. Our dinner concoction had turned out pretty good. It had been a while since any of us had eaten a real cooked meal.

Living back at the house with the guys, we rarely sat down together to eat and typically would each grab something to eat when we were hungry, eating alone in our rooms or somewhere else in the house. By the way Taya was eating, it was obvious it had been a while since she had eaten anything and I smiled at her wondering if she could even taste it.

Dinner was mostly quiet, Carter flipped through the pages of his book as he ate while Max and I stole glances at each other between bites. I thought about what he had told me in the Bronco and wished we were alone, so I could ask him about it. Did he really think about asking me to Prom or was he just teasing me like he usually did? It was so hard to tell sometimes. I must have drifted off into a daydream because when Carter spoke it almost startled me and I had to prevent myself from jumping in my seat too much.

"We can settle down for the night, but I want to get these windows painted before we try to turn any lights on or light any candles ok?"

We all nodded at what Carter had said. Leaving the dishes on the table, Taya and I grabbed a gallon of paint and got to work on the kitchen windows. There were only two so it didn't take long. There weren't enough paint brushes to go around, so I simply used my hand, dipping it in the can and then smearing it on the glass. The paint was warm and thick as it dripped all over the floor.

The color of the paint was a dark green and I joked with Taya about what place in the camp they would want to paint such a hideous green. She added that it probably was the color of the boy's bathrooms and we both laughed. It felt good to laugh and I thought to myself that it was nice to have another girl around.

After all the windows were painted over, we drew all the curtains on the windows that had them and pinned all the darkest sheets over the windows as well, leaving the lighter or white sheets for ourselves to sleep in.

"Carter, what do you think we should do about the front door?" Max asked.

"Let's carry that dresser from the bedroom over."

"Good idea."

The two men made a lot of noise moving the furniture to baracade the front door, but once they were finished and the cabin was as secure as we could get, we all started to feel a little safer. I know Taya and I both felt much better after we took turns taking the world's shortest showers. It wasn't much, but it did feel good.

After cleaning up Taya and I curled up on one couch, sharing a warm wool blanket that was in a terrible yellow and orange plaid pattern. It was itchy and had a strange odor, but it was better than nothing. I had set out all the different color polishes I had brought and Taya was busily surveying the lot, trying to decide what color she wanted.

"So… Taya," Max said, flopping down on the couch across from us. "I hear your going to go to New Mexico with us. I am glad you decided to stay. I could use another person to help keep brainiac…" he pointed over to Carter with his thumb, "and little miss troublemaker over here in line."

Taya giggled and I joined in when Max waggled his eyebrows at me. Once the laughter had subsided we all became quiet once again.

"My mother and I were on our way to New Mexico before… before you found me." Taya didn't look up when she spoke, but simply analyzed each bottle of polish like it was incredibly interesting. "We listened to the transmissions and when they stopped, we got scared. She preached that the prophecy of our destruction had begun. I thought she was crazy at first…" She was starting to struggle with her words, so I put a hand on her shoulder and she took a deep breath to calm herself.

"It's ok. You don't have to talk about it if you

don't want to. I know how you feel, I lost my parents too and Abby and Carter lost their dad." I felt my body stiffen when Max mentioned my father. That wound had not yet healed and it probably never would.

Taya nodded and began painting her fingers a very bright pink. I chose black again. It took me longer to finish than normal because I kept glancing up to watch Max by the small fire he had built, which provided just enough light. He was holding his mother's gold cross necklace in his hand while staring into the fire. He never spoke of what happened to his parents, but I knew that it was probably a subject I shouldn't bring up.

I remembered the night he had shown up at our house. There was a huge rain storm and he must have been pounding on the front door for a long while before any of us heard him. When he finally made it inside he was soaked to the bone. I watched from the stairs as my Dad and Carter spoke to Max, trying to comfort him. He didn't have to say much for us all to know what happened, the rain had not washed away all the blood on his clothes nor could it hide the tears and sorrow on his face. Never before had I seen a person look so completely broken and it hurt me to see him that way.

He must have felt my eyes on him because he looked up and quickly dropped the cross back into his pocket. I gave him a small smile in comfort, which he returned before heading over to the dining table with Carter.

"What is he writing over there?" Taya whispered to me.

"Oh, Carter? He has this book that he likes to write everything in."

"Like a journal?"

"Sort of. He writes down everything he learns about the demons, and then when we get to New Mexico we can show it to the military and maybe it will help them."

She just nodded silently and after a long silence she added, "That's a good idea. He's really smart."

"Yeah… and it helps him too. Helps him deal with everything I think."

"Did you see the size of that thing?" I overheard Max asking Carter and I wished he had said it a little more quietly. I knew instantly what he was talking about and I didn't want him to cause Taya to be on edge again. She had already come so far in such a short amount of time. She was really proving to be very strong for such a sensitive looking girl; most people would crack under such circumstances.

"Yeah, it was damn near the size of a frigging bear. Abby said Taya isn't ready to talk about it yet, but obviously the thing is strong enough to flip a van."

"True, but they must've hit it pretty hard cause it looked dead to me," Max said.

"You're probably right."

I shot them both a look that shut them up quickly, but I knew Taya had heard them. She had paused for a moment and her breath trembled, but she held it together.

Taya and I decided that we should share the bedroom and the guys were happy with getting the couches. None of us had any pajamas so we just wore what we wanted and crawled into bed. I had given Taya a clean shirt to sleep in and she had quickly fallen asleep almost as soon as she hit the pillow. It took me longer though. I was exhausted, but it seemed that as soon as I laid down, my mind just started to race with thoughts and I couldn't relax.

I tossed and turned for hours and dreamt that Max and I had gone to Prom together, but a giant beast ran through the crowd causing complete panic. People were screaming and the sounds of the demon's claws against the gymnasium floor made my skin crawl, like nails against a chalkboard.

I bolted up from sleep just when the demon was about to grab me and realized I was in the cabin. I looked over at Taya; she was twitching softly but still asleep thankfully. I tried my best to crawl gently out of bed, not wanting to disturb Taya. I crept down the hallway to take a look at Carter and Max in the living room before I went to the bathroom. Carter was sprawled wildly with his mouth hanging open, luckily he wasn't snoring. Carter could take down walls with the sound of his snores.

When I looked over into the other couch it was empty and I quickly searched for Max. Just as my heart started to thump in my chest I found him. He was slumped over in an arm chair near what remained of the fire. The embers glowed very faintly and I guessed the fire had gone out a while ago. I walked over to him and a sparkle on his hand caught my eye. His mother's necklace was wrapped around his fingers and my heart broke for him. Having to see the pain of what Taya was going through, must have brought back his own painful memories. He kept them buried inside and that burden was obviously weighting heavy on his mind.

    I pulled the wool blanket I had used earlier off the couch and draped it over Max. I wanted to hug him, to kiss him, but I was too afraid. I had known him my whole life and always considered him like my second big brother, but there was something about him. There had always been something about him that made my heart beat harder whenever I saw him. I had always been hesitant to be the one to take that first step, and see if we could be something more.

    I wanted there to be something more, but with the state of the world it made it much more difficult. I studied his strong features a moment longer before I turned to leave. His thick dark lashes cast shadows on his cheeks through the soft glow of the fire and I noticed that his lips, that I so longed to kiss, were slighted turned downward revealing the slightest hint of a frown. I realized at that moment how very much alike as well as different we were. When he started to stir I quickly retreated, not wanting to get caught looking like I'd just been staring at him.

Chapter 5

Heading back to bed from the bathroom I had thought I heard a scratching sound, but figured it was the last of the embers popping and disregarded it.

I crawled back into bed next to Taya and finally fell into a deep sleep until I felt skinny fingers clenching my arm in a death grip, shaking me very hard.

"Abby. Abby wake up."

I rolled over sleepily not wanting to be rudely removed from the sleep I just finally started to enjoy, then my eyes popped open. "Taya?"

"Abby you gotta wake up."

"What's wrong?" I asked as I grabbed a match to light a candle. The room faintly lit up in a orange glow and I saw Taya's terrified face. She looked a tiny bit relieved when I finally started to wake up even though I wasn't very happy about it.

"Something is outside," she pointed toward the window, her skinny arm shaking.

"It's probably just the wind Taya, a big storm was…" I froze when I heard it and quickly grabbed my knife that was resting on my night stand. Taya quickly scrambled to my side making small squeaking whimpers.

The sounds were getting more incessant, seemingly coming from every direction. It sounded like dozens of rodents digging into the walls.

I held my knife out in front of me waiting for some invisible attacker as we slowly backed our way out of the room. My bare legs were covered in goose bumps as the fear rippled across my skin.

"What is it Abby?" She sounded as if having me

awake would solve the problem and I would instantly know what to do. It was nice that she thought so highly of me. I was as terrified as she was, but I couldn't show it. If I did, our chances of making it out alive from whatever was about to happen would be very slim.

"I don't know. We need to go wake the guys." As I said it, a loud crash shattered the bedroom window and Taya screamed. I leaped forward and quickly pulled the door shut, slamming it hard. The pictures on the nearby walls rattled and then fell to the floor.

I felt Taya clinging onto my shirt with a death grip and decided to shove her into the bathroom knowing there was no window in there. I hoped she would be safe, but at the moment it was my only way of protecting her.

"Get in there and lock the door!" I shouted as I slammed the door behind her. I made my way quickly down the rest of the hallway as the sounds of Taya crying slowly faded away.

More windows were shattering throughout the cabin and I could hear Carter and Max yelling in the living room. I could also hear what sounded like hundreds of little feet scurrying across a wooden floor. My instinct to protect my brother and Max overcame my fear and I bolted into the living room.

"Carter! Max!" I yelled as I locked my eyes on a terrifying sight.

Small little demons about the size of a three year old child were attacking Carter and Max. They were dark, scaly looking creatures with long sharp nails and a large wide mouth holding dozens of pointy teeth. They reminded me of the gremlins I had seen in a movie once and it brought back all the childhood fears I had of the nasty things.

I was frozen in shock for a moment, but when I heard Max call my name I sprang into action.

One little demon was attacking Carter's leg, it took a swipe and made three long slices through his jeans and across his calf. He screamed out in pain and I lunged, chopping its boney arm off as it raised its scaly green arm to attack again.

It turned toward me and growled loudly, its mouth opening wider than any normal jaw bone would allow. I felt bile rise from my stomach as I watched, expecting the little demon's head to snap in half. I swallowed back the foul taste in my mouth and swung my knife at it again and it jumped out of the way. The gremlin-like demon hissed at me and grabbed its severed arm and took off out of a window.

As I watched the one armed demon leap out the window in a single bound another one of them jumped on my back and started biting my shoulder. Pain screamed through me as its dozens of tiny razor sharp teeth broke my flesh. I tried to grab it, but another one came running toward me, trying to slice up my legs with its claws. I kicked it in the face and sent it flying across the room. The sight of it slamming into a bookshelf brought a satisfied smile to my face.

I could see the guys struggling, each fighting two or three little demons crawling all over them, biting and scratching. I wanted to help them, but I was fighting my own pint sized demons. Every time I got rid of one another would take its place.

I felt warm blood dripping down my shirt, but I couldn't get the demon off my back. I struggled, flinging from side to side, hitting with my fists, but nothing worked. A thought flashed in my mind to try and stab it, but I quickly discarded that idea. They moved too quickly and it would almost be a worse fate, being killed by accidently stabbing myself than by a demon, I thought. As I swirled around I saw something on a wall and got an idea. I quickly ran for it and at the last second I twisted and landed heavily into a pair of antlers. My head smacked firmly between the large boney protrusions, but the demon on my shoulder wasn't so lucky.

It let out a loud shriek as blood dribbled out of its mouth, but let go. It went limp and hung off the wall, and I watched its dark blood drip to the floor.

Not wanting to waste any time, I turned to see Max fling one off his back and pull out his gun. I knew they had wanted to use the guns as a last resort, the bullets were hard to come by and with so many targets it would be easy to accidently harm one of us. He shot two in quick succession and their heads exploded on impact sending green gore flying.

"Abby!" Max ran to me, quickly shooting at a demon that tried to get me from behind. I was so focused on watching Max that I hadn't noticed it behind me.

"There are so many of them Max!" I looked around and it seemed that their numbers were growing rapidly as they came crawling in through the windows like roaches.

"Where's Taya?"

"I locked her in the bathroom," I said as I stabbed a demon through the top of its head as it grabbed at my leg. I was expecting to hit bone, but my knife easily penetrated its scaly flesh. I pulled out the knife and almost had to fling the sticky head of the demon off of the end of it.

More demons were running throughout the cabin, attacking us and causing chaos by breaking things or throwing objects across the room. Carter, Max and I were slowly being backed into a corner of the cabin as their numbers grew.

"There are so damn many of the little fuckers!"

"Abby, where is your gun?"

I cursed myself for leaving it in the bedroom. I wanted to grab it, but it was leaning against the wall right under a window.

Max sliced with his knife in a large sweeping motion, causing a gooey green line to form across the row of demons in front of us. They growled louder and a few dove at us. I kicked as many as I could and took off limbs and ears with my knife when I could. Carter was holding a knife in one hand and an arrow in another. Stabbing and slicing at the same time, but there were just too many of them. Several of them were fighting with missing limbs or even trying to hit us with their severed parts, throwing the scaly, stinking pieces of demon at us.

Suddenly a deafening blast rattled the room and I saw the look of shock on their ugly little faces.

I looked to my left and there was Taya, carrying my shotgun.

She cocked it again and shot at the back of the group again and the demons quickly started running for the windows, desperately trying to escape. The confidence they had felt by backing us into a corner had immediately dissipated.

We started to fight back harder and I yelled for Taya to grab us ammo. She ran for the bag in the kitchen and swung at a demon with the butt of the gun sending it flying onto the kitchen counter. The site of her running around with a shotgun and an oversized t-shirt with her skinny legs poking out the bottom, would normally have been hilarious, but at this particular moment she was nothing short of an angel to me.

"Max!" Taya yelled as she tossed a magazine at him.

He caught it, quickly loading his gun and taking out demons with every shot.

I turned and helped Carter fight off a particularly fat little demon. Its round stomach protruded so far, it was odd how it kept itself upright. We quickly overpowered it and watched as it retreated with an arrow sticking out the back of its head.

Taya shot at the last few as they tried climbing out the window, their bodies falling back into the cabin like rocks.

We all stood there in shock for a moment and I quickly fell to the floor as the adrenaline in my body ran out.

"Abby!" Carter and Max ran to me. Both their

faces riddled with scratches and green spots of demon blood and streaks of red.

"She's losing a lot of blood. Max go get the first aid kit!" I heard Carter barking orders. I turned my head to see Max, but instead I saw Taya.

Her once terrified eyes had turned defiant and I smiled at her.

"You did it Taya. You saved us."

"Yeah, good job Taya," Carter added. She smiled up at him as tears started to stream down her face.

Max quickly came back with the kit and they got to work on my shoulder. I knew the demon had bitten it, but I didn't think it could have been that bad. The looks on their faces, however, said otherwise.

"Put pressure on it Max, while I get the alcohol."

"You ready Abby?" I nodded gritting my teeth. I felt someone hold my hand and I squeezed it as Carter poured alcohol onto the wound. I tried holding it back, but I screamed loudly as the alcohol sizzled and bubbled in the open wounds.

"Ok. Ok. Worst part is over." I looked over to

Taya. It was her hand I was holding and I was grateful for her comfort. She had suddenly become so strong and brave.

"Carter, we need to get out of here," I said trying to stand up, but he pushed me back down. I didn't want to just lay there. What if the shotgun only scared them off for a moment and they would be crawling back in through the windows at any moment?

"Taya, you keep pressure on this. Max and I are going to pack up the Bronco and we are going. Don't let her sit up," Carter ordered.

Taya nodded and I saw the guys quickly moving about the cabin, jumping over or kicking out of the way any demon bodies they walked past.

"You did good." I told Taya again and she looked at me, a small smile forming on her quivering lips.

"I didn't know if I could do it, but I had to. I wasn't able to help my mom…" tears started to trickle down her cheeks with more urgency, "I was afraid of what might happen, that I would be left in that bathroom alone."

"You were brave Taya. I don't know if we would have made it without you."

I squeezed her hand and she squeezed back. We sat in silence then, while the guys finished loading up the Bronco.

"Ok, Abs. Time to go," Max said as he lifted me up and headed for the door.

I looked back over his shoulder as we walked out and tried to count the number of demons that lay lifeless on the cabin floor. I got to seventeen before he was walking down the steps and I squeezed my eyes shut not wanting to see their ugly bodies any longer.

Carter had backed the Bronco right up to the cabin and we all quickly got in before he went speeding out of the camp.

The sky was starting to turn a pretty orange. It was morning. Max laid my head onto his lap as I fell into a deep sleep. After a night like that I would have expected to have a nightmare, but I had the most pleasant dream. Max and I were at my favorite amusement park, Silverwood. Carter and Taya were there too and we were all heading to get in line for

Tremors. It was a classic wood coaster and one of the scariest rides I had ever been on, but being at that amusement park were some of my happiest memories of my childhood.

When I woke up, panic instantly coursed through me. I was in the Bronco alone, and we were stopped on the side of the road. Just as I felt my heart begin to pound I saw a familiar face and my fear melted away.

"Hey, sleepy head!" Max said.

I saw him leaning against a guard rail, eating a can of pork and beans. "You hungry?" he asked, offering me the can.

"No thanks," I said as I crawled out of the Bronco. Pork and beans looked to be one of Max's favorite post demon apocalypse meals, but I just couldn't stomach the stuff.

Plus my whole body was sore, especially my shoulder and I just wasn't in the mood for food even thought I could feel my stomach rumbling.

"Where are we?" I asked.

"Just outside of Utah. How are you feeling?" Max walked over to inspect my bandages. "Looks like these need changing."

I closed my eyes as Max peeled away the bandage. I always thought it was easier to bear when I wasn't looking.

"Well it's looking better. I think I did a pretty good job, what do you think?"

I hesitated for a moment and then looked down at my shoulder and saw my wound. I had to admit he did do a good job. It looked clean and he had a row of butterfly bandages to hold it together nicely. It wasn't as scary looking as I had expected it to be.

"Looks good. Thanks Max."

He smiled and started to smear antibiotic on it before adding fresh gauze. I watched him as he worked. His brow furrowed as he concentrated, taking extra care to cause me the least amount of pain as possible.

When he was done he looked up and caught me staring at him. "Geez, Abs. You really scared the hell out of me and everyone for that matter," he said letting out a breath.

"Sorry," I looked away and pulled the sleeve of my shirt back on.

"No, no. Don't look away. Don't ever look away."

He grabbed my face and suddenly kissed me hard. His warms lips sent shivers down my spine as my mind whirled with shock, confusion and then pleasure. We explored each other as he held me close to his body and I felt myself give in to him.

"Oh my gosh! I'm sorry." Max and I both turned just in time to see the back of Taya retreating behind the Bronco.

I felt my face flush as we released each other, but Max lingered for a moment brushing stray strands of hair out of my face.

"Has she woken up yet? Hey, what's going on?" Carter's eyes danced back and forth between us.

"He was just checking my shoulder Carter." I knew how protective my brother was of me and I didn't want to give him any reason to get worked up. We have enough problems as it is and Carter has quite a temper when given cause and my kissing his best friend was enough cause, I was sure of it.

"Oh ok, you're looking better Abby. You get

something to eat? Max get her something to eat." As Max walked to the trunk while rolling his eyes, Carter grabbed me in a bear hug, but quickly released when he felt me flinch in pain. "Sorry Abby. You scared the hell out of me back there, you know that?"

"Well I didn't mean to Carter," I sighed. It's not like I had meant to get bitten so badly by that demon, but I knew Carter wasn't really trying to chastise me, he was just really worried.

"I can't lose you Abby." He put his hand on my good shoulder and I saw the fear in his eyes. I knew my brother loved me, but it was nice to see such brotherly love from him.

"I'm ok now. That was just a close call." I tried to reassure him.

"Well, I don't know how many close calls I can take."

"Me neither," Max added as he handed me a can of pineapples and a bottled water.

I took a seat against the guard rail and ate, while everyone else decided what we should do next. Taya and Carter seemed to be getting along nicely and I was starting to think she might have a crush on him.

"I think we should stay on I15 as planned. It is the most direct route," Carter said.

"I agree with Carter," Taya added a little too eagerly. Carter's chest seemed to puff up a little at having someone agree with him, and I was sure he had no idea of Taya's feelings.

"That will take us right through Salt Lake City. That's a highly populated area. You don't think we should try to avoid it? Maybe there is another way around, how about this?" Max pointed to a place on the map.

"No that won't work, it's almost too isolated." Carter explained. "If something were to go wrong, we would have no where to go. Besides I think its been proven that it doesn't matter if the area is populated or not."

"He has a point," I added trying not to let my gaze linger on Max for too long. He was just so hot I couldn't help myself. "So are we ready to go?"

"We need gas," Taya announced while holding up a long hose for display.

"Not it!" I called out quickly before downing the rest of my water.

"Don't worry, Carter lost the bet already so he has to do it," Taya said with a smile. She tossed him the hose without warning and Carter juggled it in his hands before catching it.

"Oh really?" I looked over to Carter with my eyebrows raised and he just waived me off.

"Now are we ready to go?" he asked.

Taya saw my questioning look and answered it, "There is a street a few blocks down that have quite a few cars. We are going to head there and see what we can find. Do you want to stay here?" She asked, letting the question hang in there and flashing her eyes in Max's direction quickly.

"Oh." My cheeks started to blush realizing she was trying to give Max and me an opportunity to be alone. "No, I need to stretch my legs a bit. It's not far, I'll go with you."

"Then it's settled." Carter grabbed our empty gas can, tossed it to Max and closed up the Bronco as we started to head down the street.

It was early afternoon and the sun was starting to warm things up. I felt naked without my shotgun, but I needed to let my shoulder heal and carrying that heavy gun wasn't going to help any. Max had offered to carry it before we left when he saw me glance at it longingly. I declined when I saw he was already carrying a backpack of water bottles and the gas cans. Carter, of course, carried nothing but his book and the knife strapped to his leg, which I was fairly sure he had forgotten about.

"So why do you think this all happened?" Taya asked completely out of the blue, directing the question toward Carter.

"Huh? You asking me?" She nodded at him. "Well there are lots of theories really. Some people believe God is punishing us, some believe they are aliens taking over our planet, some..."

"What do you believe?" Taya interrupted.

"Honestly I am not concerned about the how or why. I just want them gone."

We all nodded silently at that. Trying to understand why this was happening or how, was just too much to fathom. All our minds could really think about was survival. Even if we did figure out why this was all happening, what could four small town teenagers really do about it? Either scenario had ominous outcomes for us.

We had to try four different cars before we found one with any gas left.

"Damn! That was a lot worse than I thought it would be." Carter wiped his face with his sleeve after vomiting. He had nearly puked all over Taya's sneakers, but she jumped out the way with a squeal.

"That house is really creeping me out," Max said as he screwed the top onto one of the gas cans.

"Which one? That blue one?" Carter questioned pointing to a small one story house.

"Yeah, I could have sworn I saw someone peeking through the blinds," Max said.

"What?" Taya's mouth fell open in shock and she ducked behind Carter. He looked at her a bit confused and turned back toward the house. I thought her reaction was a little dramatic, but she was young.

"Should we go check it out?" Max asked.

"Don't look at me. I don't want anything to do with this." I put my hands up in the air like I was surrendering and took a step back. I saw Max smirk at me as he set the gas cans by my feet.

"Ok then, you ladies stay here. We will go check it out." Max tried to sound gallant, but I could tell he was half sincere and half trying to be a smartass.

"Here we go," Taya said under her breath while she flopped into the empty driver's seat of a nearby car. I watched her as she bit at her nails and wished I had brought my radio; it had been a while since I tried to hear if the transmission was playing and I was desperate to try it.

Chapter 6

"Are there keys in that car Taya?"

"How should I know?"

"Will you look please?" She rolled her eyes and looked about the front seat.

"Nope, no keys. What the heck do you want keys for?" She asked keeping her eyes on Carter as he approached the house.

"Nothing, forget it." I was starting to get tired and dug into the pack Max left on the street for a bottle of water. I chugged the warm water as I watched Carter and Max disappear into the front yard of the house.

We were in a typical rural neighborhood, but this house stood out like a sore thumb amongst the rest, even during a demon apocalypse.

The entire property was lined with a four foot high brick wall and appeared to still be currently worked on, and the more I started to look, the more I realized that the cars were positioned in such a manner as to look like barricades. They were all placed closely together, and I guessed that was to prevent a demon hound from getting around them easily. This house was some sort of fortress of some sort. At the thought of the hounds I sniffed at the air, just to be sure there weren't any nearby even though if there were we would have known already. Their overpowering stench was hard to miss.

"What do you think is taking them so long?" Taya asked sounding impatient. I noticed that she had given up biting her nails and reverted to pacing.

"You sure seem worked up. What's the matter? They know what they are doing, even if it doesn't seem like it." I tried to make light of the situation and I wasn't sure if I was trying to convince Taya or myself. That was always Max's tactic and it seemed to work for him most of the time.

"I just have a bad feeling. Don't you? It's too quiet. I can't stand this waiting, I am going to go check on them."

"What? No Taya, wait. Shit!" I knew I was going to have to go after her and I really didn't want to. She had already made it to the yard before I had even started to move. I could see her black-haired head moving around behind the brick wall.

"Are you insane? You can't just go stomping around like that," I said as I ran up near the entrance to the yard just a few feet from where Taya stood.

"Ssshh!" She snapped around and pointed along the side of the house. I jogged the few feet to her side and tried to see where she was pointing.

"I don't see anything."

"Right there." She shook her first finger toward what she was pointing at. Along the back wall of the house, I could barely make out what looked like a sliver of a door. "It looks like an open door. They must have gone inside."

Taya scurried ahead before I could protest and held the door open wider for me to see. A triumphant smile grew on her face as I approached. "See… I told you Abby."

I bit my tongue when I wanted to snap at her and pulled out my knife before entering the room ahead of her. There was no way I was going to let her lead the way if there was some sort of demon waiting inside to kill us. I could at least fight it off and maybe even kill it, I had already killed one, but Taya wouldn't stand a chance.

The room we entered was a standard laundry room, but the fresh scent of detergent alarmed me. A folded stack of towels was on top of the dryer.

"Someone is here," Taya said sniffing the towels and sighing deeply.

"Do you hear that?"

"Hear what?"

"Voices. I think I hear voices. That sounds like Carter." I rushed out of the laundry room and into a hallway. I turned to the left toward what I thought were the sounds of Carter. Taya trailed behind me clinging to a towel.

When I reached the living room I was in complete shock. Carter and Max were seated in a gaudy flowery orange couch and standing in front of them was a very pissed off looking old man holding a rifle. I guessed he was in his late sixties, but his face was layered in wrinkles giving it a permanent scowl.

The sight of me seemed to have caught him off guard for a moment, but when he saw Taya come barreling in behind me with one of his towels in tow, his face became red.

"I thought you boys said you were alone?" His voice was deep and scruffy, like he'd spent too many years smoking.

"You little thieves were trying to pull a fast one on me weren't ya?"

"We aren't thieves!" Taya blurted.

"Oh really? What is that you got in your hand then, kid? Is that towel yours? I suppose you were trying to sneak up behind me?" He said eyeing my knife.

"No." I slid the knife back into my pant leg. "Listen, we were just worried about them when they didn't come back, so we went looking for them that's all."

I tried to inch my way closer to the couch and Taya followed, still clinging onto her stolen towel.

"No, you kids listen. You think you can sneak in here and steal from an old man! Isn't the world in a bad enough state?"

"I didn't mean to steal it." Taya stepped closer to him, offering the towel. "It just smelled so good and clean. It just… just reminded me of my mom. That's all."

I saw his face start to soften a bit and I knew this was our chance. I tried to telepathically tell Taya to keep it up; we needed this man to feel sorry for us. I knew it was hard for her to speak of her mother, but if that's what would get us out of this mess then that is what had to be done.

"She used the same detergent," Taya said sounding much like a little child. He looked down at the towel and then at her.

"You can keep it."

Taya's face instantly lit up and she hugged it like it was a teddy bear.

"Ah hell," He said lowering his rifle and I saw Max and Carter start to relax. They each released a deep breath and I tried to curse them each out for being so stupid, hoping that they could read lips.

"What are you kids doing?"

"We are trying to get to New Mexico. We heard a transmission that there is a safe zone there." Taya blurted out like she was telling someone she knew well. I thought that I was going to have to yell at her too. We couldn't go around telling every crazy person we found what we were doing. We didn't even know this man.

"That transmission cut out weeks ago kid, what are you going there for?"

"There are still people there," Carter quickly corrected him. "They just don't have the power to run the transmissions anymore. They are still there."

"You're grasping at straws kid," The old man said as he settled down in an arm chair. "Go ahead sit down you two, I ain't gonna bite ya."

Taya and I sat on the couch with Carter and Max. Fear was starting to trickle through me, causing the hairs on my arms to stand on end. My biggest fear was exactly what this old man was saying. There was no one left in New Mexico. My urge to find a radio grew even stronger. Hearing the transmission was our only way to know for sure that we were making the right choice. That we hadn't come all this way for nothing.

"How do you know that no one is there?" Max asked after looking at me and realizing the fear written plainly on my face.

"They ain't playing the transmissions any more are they? Isn't that proof enough for ya?"

"Obviously not," Carter said with disdain. I knew he didn't want to be wrong. That we had risked our lives to make this journey for nothing. He had promised us all that going there was our only way to stay safe, that it was the only way we would survive. It was because of his urging that we left home. I didn't want to think of what Carter would do if he was wrong.

"Look, sir."

"You can call me Charlie."

"Look Charlie," I said. "We are just passing through. We didn't mean you any harm. We can just leave and be out of your way."

I looked to the others and started to sit up. "Ya'll wanna stay for lunch?"

"Huh?"

"Listen, I haven't seen much of anyone since… since, it happened. I've got plenty. Why don't you stay and have lunch? Maybe I can talk some sense into you kids."

At that, he rose from his seat and headed to his kitchen. We all looked at each other and everyone just shrugged. He seemed nice enough, now that we got things cleared up, and it would be crazy to turn down food.

Carter stayed on the couch with his arms crossed over his chest and Taya stayed with him making comments about the living room. She was particularly interested in a photo of a kid at a circus and went into a long discussion about how much she liked going to the circus, and how she hoped she would get to go to one again someday and maybe Carter could take her.

It was obvious none of this was sinking in, but he was nodding his head like he was listening so she just kept chattering away. I envied her ability to be so cheerful, but I guessed that was her defense mechanism. She had chosen to overlook the way things were and pretend everything was ok. I couldn't blame her; she had been through some pretty rough things. Watching your mother get eaten by giant demon birds has to screw up a person's head. I hadn't had to witness my father's passing, but the loss of him would haunt me every day the rest of my life.

"You kids like Spaghetti O's?" Charlie asked holding up a giant can of it. We spent the next hour sitting around Charlie's dining table talking and eating.

"So you came out and just shot all the little buggers?" Charlie asked Taya. "That's pretty impressive for such a twig of a girl."

"I'm not a twig!" Taya said defiantly and we all laughed.

"Charlie, you said you had a radio, does it work?" I asked. I was dying to check and see if the transmissions were back on.

"Sure, but you're not gonna hear nothing, but static."

"I'd like to try any way if that's ok with you?" He considered it for a moment and nodded.

"Sure kid." Charlie slowly stood up with a grunt and walked to a back room as I followed. I looked back and saw Carter whispering something into Max's ear and Max shook his head solemly.

I could tell Carter didn't much like Charlie, but that was only because he didn't agree with him. Carter was stubborn like that. He didn't want to be wrong and he didn't want anyone to question him. No matter how much we all warmed up to Charlie, I could tell it only irritated Carter further.

It was nice to have the escape though. To sit around a table and talk and laugh, like things were normal. I silently prayed that once we made it to New Mexico we could spend all our evenings like this. Just hanging out, chatting and having a good meal together.

Charlie slid into a squeaky desk chair and pushed open the lid of an antique wooden roll top desk. It was a beautiful large mahogany desk, with intricate carvings decorating the sides and trim of the piece.

"That's a very pretty desk," I commented.

"It was my wife's." He touched the wood lovingly. "I always hated it. The damn thing weights a ton. She always insisted that we take it with us wherever we moved, but I always wanted to sell it. Now, I don't know if I could ever part with it."

Charlie turned the knob on an old radio and turned it toward me.

"There you go kid." He rose from his seat and offered it to me.

I sat down gingerly and started to play with the dials trying every station I could. I faintly remember hearing him say, good luck as he left the room.

After unsuccessfully finding anything on the radio I closed the desk and left the room. Max and Taya were seated back in the living room with Charlie, but Carter was no where in sight.

"Where's Carter?"

"He's headed back for the Bronco."

"You let him go alone?" I couldn't believe how careless the two of them were being.

"He wanted to," Taya added sounding hurt.

"He was a little upset, with this one here." Charlie said pointing to Taya. "She asked if I wanted to come with you."

"Oh," I added a little surprised. "So what did you say?"

Charlie chuckled and said, "Don't look so shocked kid. I thought about it for a moment, but I'm not leaving. This is my house, has been for over thirty years."

"I think he's crazy for staying." Max added sitting up from the couch and pulling a bag onto his shoulder.

"What's that?" I asked pointing to the bag.

"Oh I just gave you kids a few things I thought you could use," Charlie said and winked at us as we walked to the front door.

"Thanks for everything." Taya hugged Charlie quickly and walked briskly out of the house.

I wasn't going to hug him, but I was grateful for all he had done for us. He noticed my hesitation and extended his hand. "You kids be careful, ok? If you get there, and get that transmission going again, maybe I'll come see ya."

I doubted that he would but I shook his hand and we said our *thank yous* before exiting.

"So Carter really got *that* pissed?" I asked as we made our way to the gas cans. One of them was missing so I figured Carter had grabbed it on his way out. Max picked the remaining can up and we heading back toward the Bronco.

Taya took the lead, looking eager to either get back to Carter or the Bronco, I couldn't tell which.

"He's not mad at you, ya know?" Max told Taya. "He just thought that guy was going to try to talk us out of going. Tell us to go back home. He got really paranoid, thinking we were going to turn against him."

I started to laugh at that. "Turn against him? We're family. He can be such a stubborn ass sometimes."

Taya shot me a nasty glare and I raised my hands up in surrender, giggling all the while. Max started to laugh too which made her even madder.

"What's got her panties in a bunch?" Max asked.

"I think she has a little crush on Carter."

"I do not!"

We laughed some more, "Geez, ok. Keep it down, you don't have to yell." I didn't want to have her be too upset with us so I tried my best to force my smile away.

"If you two can be together, why can't Carter and I?" she asked. She stopped and turned to face us with her hands on her boney hips.

"Taya, were not…" I looked to Max and he was avoiding my eyes, squinting into the distance at the Bronco that was far ahead. I knew he was dying to hear how I answered this accusation. His lips were quivering and I could tell he was desperately trying not to smile.

"Don't try to lie Abby. I saw you two, not that I care that you were sucking face, but don't try to deny it. I see how you look at each other."

I blushed at that and quickly tried to hide it by taking a small step away from Max. I wasn't ashamed about how I felt for him, but it was so new. The kiss we shared was something I never thought would happen and I hadn't figured out what Max and I were now that it had.

"That's different Taya. Carter is…" I didn't want to tell her that I didn't think he was interested in her cause I didn't want to hurt her feelings. I could see in her eyes how much she was holding back. I was a bit taken aback by how much I realized she liked him.

"He's just a bit older than you, that's all we're trying to say." Max added.

"Oh. Well, don't worry about that. I've dated lots of guys older than me. My last boyfriend was seventeen."

"We just don't want you to get hurt." I added trying to sound supportive and it worked.

Taya softened and headed toward the Bronco again, almost with a skip in her step.

"Poor Carter," Max chuckled. "He has no clue what he is in for."

Max and I continued the short walk to the Bronco in silence, just enjoying each others company. I had inched my way closer to Max's side as we walked and I could tell we were probably closer than necessary by the look on Carter's face when we made it to the Bronco.

The more my feelings for Max grew and the more I dreamt that my chance of being with him was possible, I started to care less and less if my brother knew about us.

Carter quickly grabbed the gas can out of Max's hand and filled up the Bronco while the rest of us crawled in. Taya insisted on sitting shotgun, so Max and I gladly sat in the back. As we made our way into Utah the terrain slowly began to change.

"So what did he give you?" I asked Max randomly, trying to break the awkward silence.

"Who, Charlie?" Carter groaned as he heard the name. "He gave us food mostly, some soaps, oh, and he wanted you to have this." Max dug into a side pocket and pulled out a small radio. It was not much bigger than my hand and the antennae was broken, but it brought a big smile to my face. "He said that he hopes we find what we are looking for, and doesn't want us to give up."

"Wow. That's nice of him." I sounded more appreciative that I should have, but that was probably the most thoughtful gift I had received in ages.

"That guy is full of crap. We *will* find what we

are looking for and we are going to win this." Carter held up his book. "We've got so much information. We're going to give it to the military and it's going to make a difference, just you wait and see."

"I believe you Carter," I added. "No one is saying that they don't. You don't need to be so defensive."

"Me too. I never doubted you," Taya added while squeezing his shoulder.

I could tell that recent events had really shaken Carter and he was starting to lose hope, but I wasn't sure of what I could do to raise his sprits. The only thing that would truly matter was getting to safety in New Mexico and we were still a long ways away.

As it got darker, our surroundings became more and more populated. I knew the gas we had gotten wouldn't get us far and we would have to stop again soon. Carter realized this too and we pulled into a gas station to try the pumps.

Max went inside the store to turn on the pumps while we each tried a nozzle. Taya's was working, so we pulled the Bronco to pump number eight and were able to almost fill it up.

With that small victory we all made our way into the convenience store, scouring the aisles for any hidden treasures. I noticed Max pulled a door closed near the back of the store and I smiled at him. That was good thinking on his part. The last thing we needed was a demon to come barreling out of a back room again. I realized that I had become less vigilant of my surroundings since I was hurt, and silently vowed I would be more observant.

In the end we had all carried what we found back to the Bronco and pigged out.

"Wow, I never knew Funyons were so good," Taya said with a mouthful.

"Yeah, I can't believe you never had any before. They are the best," Carter added. Food seemed to have lightened his mood.

"Where do you think we should stay for the night?" I asked taking an over eager bite out of a power bar. I normally would stick my tongue out at the thought of having to eat one, but I quickly realized that they weren't so bad. The texture was a little off, but I liked it anyway.

"Maybe we can find a nice house to stay in?" Taya asked excitedly.

"Yeah, that sounds like a good idea. What do you two think?"

"Sounds good," Max said inaudibly. His mouth was packed full of stale Pringles. We passed around a two liter bottle of Mountain Dew that we found and all took a swig. It was flat and a good while past the expiration date, but after a few test sips we deemed it edible.

"How about those houses?" I pointed to what looked like newly developed homes that were visible down the street from the gas station.

"As good a place as any," Max said.

Chapter 7

Carter let Taya pick the house and she chose a beautiful two-story, complete with a white picket fence and shutters on the windows. Even though the garden out front was dead, I could imagine what the place looked like in all its splendor with the rose bushes in full bloom.

After the guys made a thorough inspection they deemed it safe and we entered. A tiled foyer led to a large staircase that was lined with family pictures.

Although it was certain the family in those pictures would never return to their home, I still had a feeling that we were intruding.

"Wow, this place is gorgeous." Taya's eyes lit up as she eyed the expensive furniture and décor. I was different however, the fancier a place was, the less comfortable I felt. I liked a house that looked lived in, not a place that had to have everything in its proper place. I saw a picture of a beautiful woman, whose eyes looked down at me from over a slightly pointy nose, half expecting her to snap at me for walking on her carpet with my shoes on.

"Come on Abby, let's go check upstairs." Taya grabbed my hand and nearly dragged me up the stairs behind her. She opened doors, peeking into rooms, calling out in her too chipper voice what they were.

"Looks like this one is a guys bedroom. Ooh wait, look at those double doors, I bet that is the master bedroom."

We opened the doors and walked into the master suite. A large king sized bed dominated the room, still freshly made with hideously floral sheets. The four wooden posts of the bed were obnoxiously carved and it occurred to me that these people bought things just because they were expensive and not necessarily because they looked good.

"Wow, these people had terrible taste. Look at these curtains." I stuck my tongue out as I tugged at the drapes.

"I like it. This place looks like it came straight out of magazine. Wow, Abby look at this closet."

It took some digging but I found some plain shirts and jeans buried in the back. Taya went straight for the designer threads, trying things on and twirling around in front of the mirror.

"I don't know how you do it?"

"Do what? Look totally awesome in these boots?" she asked displaying her leg and the almost knee high leather boots she put on over a pair of skinny jeans.

"I don't know how you can act like nothing happened." I didn't mean to be a mood killer, but I blurted the words out before I could stop myself.

"What do you want me to do Abby? Mope around and be sad all the time like you? My mom used to tell me all the time that I could be upset all I wanted about something, but it wouldn't change anything. Get it? I can be sad and depressed, and believe me I am, but what is that going to do for me? Nothing." She walked over to me and unzipped the boots handing them to me. "You gotta let things go. If you are just going to be sad all the time, you are going to forget what it is you are fighting for."

I stared at the boots she held dangling in front of my face and grabbed them. "You have a point." I wasn't too proud to admit it and for the first time in a long time, I let go of all the grief and fear that consumed me.

We spent the next hour laughing as we tried on ridiculous outfits. The clothes fit Taya better than myself, as their previous owner was closer to her height. I, however, was a good few inches taller than Taya and tried on a few of the male blazers in the closet as we laughed hysterically at our mirrored images, until we turned to see Carter and Max looking at us like we were two crazy people.

"You're right Carter," Max said simply, "She has

completely lost it. This is definitely irregular behavior."

The two of them were trying their damnedest not to smile, but giant grins stretched across their faces as they pointed at Taya and me. They suddenly burst into hysterical laughter until their faces turned red and for a moment I thought for sure that Carter was going to pee himself from laughing so hard.

"I don't think they like our outfits," I said eyeing Taya who was hidden under a giant brimmed hat and wearing a very ridiculous ball gown.

"You know what Abby, I think your right." An evil grin crept onto her face and we both nodded to each other as we bolted for the giant bed and started the biggest pillow fight we had ever had.

When I landed a particularly hard blow on the back of Max's behind that sent feathers flying everywhere, it only further encouraged the battle. Within ten minutes we had completely exhausted ourselves and we all lay in a feathery heap on the bed and giggled at the same time, the laughter slowly dying away.

"I can't remember the last time I laughed that

hard," Carter said holding his side.

Taya added, "Me neither, my cheeks hurt."

Later that night we all did our part in securing the house for the night and decided to all share the huge bed in the master suite. The guys took the outer edges of the bed, squeezing Taya and me in the middle. It was the safest I had felt since our trip started and I was hopeful that I might actually get some decent sleep.

"Abby, you awake?" Max asked in the middle of the night.

"I am now. What's up?"

"I just wanted to say that I am sorry for earlier. You know, for kissing you."

"Oh." I could feel a knot growing in my stomach at the thought that he hadn't meant to kiss me and was now regretting it. "No apology needed. Good night Max," I said in a sharp whisper. I cursed myself for letting my feelings for him show so easily, I should have known it was too good to be true. Guys like him didn't date girls like me, they dated cheerleaders or models. I was just a tomboy, and his best friend's little sister. What was I thinking?

"Don't be mad Abs. I didn't mean it like that."

I rolled over to face him and saw the bags under his eyes. He had obviously been up most of the night trying to decide what he should say to me. Trying to think of how to let me down easy I thought. "Well, how did you mean it?"

The faint light of the moon bathed his face in a white glow and I found myself staring into his deep brown eyes. They danced around under his unnaturally long lashes as he sought to find the words to what he wanted to say and at that moment the last chains of my restraint gave way. I knew he didn't feel the same way about me, but if he was going to break it off before it even started I wanted to lay everything on the table.

"You know what Max, I don't forgive you and I'm not sorry we did it either." His face looked shocked, but he didn't say anything so I rolled over, pulling my body closer to Taya trying to get as far away from his as I could. I was proud that I had finally told him the truth of how I felt for once.

A strong arm curled around my waist and Max pulled me to him. I could feel the weight of his body on me and his warm breath on my neck as he leaned in close, lightly pressing his lips against my ear.

"I hate it when you're mad at me."

I didn't say anything at first as my mind raced to decipher what was happening. Shivers shot down my spine and my entire body felt filled with electricity.

I was in a bed, wrapped in Max's arms. Other than the fact that we were sharing the bed with two other people it felt as amazing as I had always thought it would, but I never imagined I would be mad at him at the same time. We were always like that, always baiting each other, always testing and teasing, but things were different now. It mattered to me how he felt more than I wanted to admit.

"Look at me Abs." I rolled over onto my back and our eyes locked. I felt like he towered over me as my body seemed to shrink against him. "I don't regret kissing you either. I've been wanting to do it for a long time."

He stroked my face and we just held each other in silence for a long moment, our bodies tangled. There were so many thoughts flowing through my head in an emotional tidal wave, but I ignored them all. I just wanted to enjoy this moment as long as I possibly could. I felt my eyes getting heavy as a sense of ease took over me that I had not felt in a long time. I burrowed my body deeper into Max's embrace as I closed my eyes. He squeezed me tight and kissed my forehead. I then slept the best night's sleep I had in over six months.

"You two love birds want to wake up?" I heard a cheerful voice ask with a bit of a giggle.

I opened my eyes to see Taya sitting indian-style on the far edge of the bed, her two hands overflowing with feathers and she smiled evilly as she tossed them at us. A rainfall of white floated onto us. I tried to sit upright, but a heavy arm held me down. I looked over to see Max's face buried into my shoulder. He looked so peaceful; I didn't want to wake him. I slowly pulled his arm off me and slithered out of bed.

Taya watched me silently, a tiny smirk planted firmly on her face. I looked at her, raising my eyebrows, "What?"

"Oh nothing," she smiled larger, "you two just look awfully comfy for not being a couple."

I thought back about last night and the feel of Max's breath against my neck, the sensation his soft lips sent across my skin and I could feel myself blush.

"Oh my gosh!" Taya squeeled as she lept off the bed. "You gotta tell me everything. I can see it in your eyes, something happened!"

I was reluctant at first, but it became quickly apparent that she wasn't going to leave me alone until I told her every detail, not even when I wanted to go to the bathroom.

"Wow, that's so romantic," she said dreamily, surveying her reflection in the mirror. I was hesitant at first, but the details of the night were so monumental to me it was hard to hold in. It felt so good to be able to say out loud to someone how I felt about Max. Before everything happened, if I had told any of my girlfriends they would have immediately told the first person they saw even if they were vowed to secrecy. Before the day was over the whole school would have known, so I had always kept my lips sealed about my secret feelings for Max.

After getting dressed, Taya demanded she do my

hair, so I let her. It saved me the trouble of having to deal with the tangled mess anyway. She styled it in two French braids parted down the middle, and I had to admit to her what a good job she had done. She beamed with pride and I could tell she thoroughly enjoyed herself. I guessed this is what it would have felt like to have a sister.

Leaving the bathroom, I saw the empty bed and was a bit disappointed. I had wanted to talk to Max before we approached Carter, but I knew it was too late. Taya had told me that the sound of Carter cursing and noisily leaving the room is what woke her up. She said she had done her best to try talking to him. He had refused to tell her what his problem was, so she came in to wake us up herself. I was grateful that it was her and not Carter who had done it, because I was sure it would not have been feathers that were thrown at us.

I know Carter had sensed my crush on Max before, when I was around Taya's age, but he had firmly told me that Max was trouble. Max was known for having many girlfriends and none of them lasting for very long, and I knew Carter was just looking out for me. Not wanting his little sister to be just another notch in Max's belt.

Making our way into the kitchen I was greeted with the smell of something delicious. Max was manning a small camping stove I had guessed he had found somewhere in the house and was flipping giant pancakes onto a plate.

He smiled at me as I entered. "I made breakfast. You hungry?"

"Starving. How did you manage to make pancakes?"

"Magic," He said while plopping two steaming pancakes onto my plate. "I found Tang too." He pointed to a pitcher of juice on the bar.

There wasn't any butter, but there was syrup, so I drowned my pancakes in it and took a large bite. "Wow, Max, these are really good." He smiled and continued cooking. I admired him for a moment and continued eating. Being in such an expensive looking kitchen with granite countertops and stainless appliances it was funny to see Max using such a simple looking hot plate, but it suited him. Max was a man's man, and like me, fancy digs like this huge house didn't seem to fit our character.

When I was done I asked, "Where's Carter?"

"He's in the garage. Don't worry, I talked to him." Max glanced at me with the same look in his eyes as he usually had. I wasn't sure what I was expecting, I thought things would feel different now between us but they didn't.

"Oh." I wasn't quite sure if I wanted to know what they had talked about so I asked, "What's he doing in the garage?"

"Well, when he woke up he went looking around the house. Found some useful stuff in the garage."

"Like what?"

"Like....a really powerful radio." He looked up at me from the corner of his eye waiting to see my reaction.

"A what?" I said choking down the rest of my Tang. "A radio? Seriously? Does it work?" I couldn't believe he hadn't told me as soon as I walked into the kitchen. I almost wanted to snap at him for it, but I was too excited about the thought of hearing the transmission again.

"He hasn't gotten it to work, but it looks like whoever was living here was listening. They rigged it up to be more powerful, so they could pick up the signal better. Carter thinks they probably heard the transmission and left."

"Holy crap!" I hopped off the bar stool and headed toward the direction I thought might be the garage and looked back to Max for confirmation. He nodded and turned off the hot plate to join me.

I entered the garage to find Carter and Taya deep in concentration, trying to figure out how to get the radio started. It looked like the previous tenants had raided a radio station. There were several black boxes stacked on top of each other, full of dials and knobs. There were large ear phones, wires crisscrossed every which way in a tangled heap on the cold concrete floor of the garage. I noticed a CB radio was also set up. A dial displaying the signal power was stuck at zero.

"Hey guys!" Taya said as she saw us enter the garage.

"Hey. So you two get this thing started?"

"No, it's hooked up to some kind of generator,

but we think it's out of power. Carters thinking about hooking it up to the car battery and see if that would work."

"It could work." Carter added. "Or I'll electrocute myself to death. What do you think Abby?"

"Well..." I looked around the garage and saw the car battery they were talking about. It was in an old sports car, by the looks of it I guessed the previous owner was in the process of trying to restore it. "Looks pretty questionable; look at all the corrosion." I pointed my finger and Max leaned to get a better view. "What's wrong with the generator?"

"We don't know, just can't get it to start."

"Did you check if it needed gas?" I probably sounded like a smartass for asking, but guys didn't always check the most obvious of solutions to problems sometimes.

"Yes, we checked that. I think it's just burnt out, it's really old," Carter said.

"Where is it?" I asked.

"Over there," Carter pointed to a far wall while checking that all the wires were securely plugged it.

"Carter you might wanna back off for a sec," I said while I flipped the switch for the generator. I stood and watched it for a second while nothing happened and Max joined me, squatting down to watch the gauge on the front.

"Stand back Abs." Max used his arm to push me back a few steps and then swiftly kicked the generator as hard as he could.

"What the hell Max!" Carter yelled running to the generator.

"Watch out dude!" Carter tried to shove Max out of the way again, but not before Max got one more good kick at it.

"What the hell do you think you're doing?" Carter started to shout, but was cut off at the sound of the generator sputtering to life.

"It worked, it really fucking worked." Max laughed and turned around to hug me and swing me around as Carter was frozen in shock. I couldn't tell what bothered him more; the fact that I was wrapped in Max's arms or the fact that Max had actually fixed the generator by kicking it. The crazed look in his eye quickly dissolved as the hum of the generator filled the garage.

"Your welcome," Max said sarcastically as Carter rushed to the radio and I followed, being equally as excited about the possibility of hearing the transmission.

I watched him like a hawk as Carter started flipping switches and turning knobs, lights flickered to life while others blinked steadily. Taya was eager to help, taking orders from Carter on pointing the antennae this way or that.

At first it was nothing but static, and we all held our breathes in an attempt to better hear any tiny bit of transmission that might make it through.

"Did you hear that?" Carter asked slightly turning a few knobs. Just below the buzz of static we could faintly hear a voice. The same voice we had heard in our house so many weeks ago.

"They are still there!" Carter said with a deep sigh. "I told you Abby. Everything is going to be ok." It was almost impossible to know what they were saying, but we had listened to it so many times it was engraved into memories. We all repeated along quietly as the message played faintly through the static, *"This is Staff Sergeant Richardson, of the U.S. Marines, at Holloman Air Force Base in New Mexico. We can promise shelter, safety, food and water for all those who come here. This is the resistance, you are not alone. There is hope."*

Carter got up to face me. I could see tears building in his eyes. We all hugged, silently cheering at this faint symbol of hope.

Filled with a renewed sense of hope we quickly got ready to leave. Taya and I raided the pantry, finding mostly food that I didn't want to eat, *even* during an apocalypse. There were containers of caviar, fancy crackers, some bottles of wine and lots of jars of olives. I had located a small section in the pantry that must have been allotted to the children of the house and was able to snag more tang and easy mac. It was expired, but I was fairly certain that powdered cheese could last well past the expiration date.

"You girls ready?" Carter asked as we made our way into the living room.

"Yep. I call shotgun!" Taya called as she

walked briskly through the front door.

Chapter 8

We quickly settled in for a long day of driving and Taya insisted we play twenty questions to help pass the time. I was certain it was just a ploy for her to get to know more about my brother. However, Carter was quickly able to manipulate it, into a game of recalling significant details about the demons we had seen. He had not had a chance to detail much about the small gremlin-like demons we had seen at the camp and he was chomping at the bit, so he had enlisted Taya to write the information down. As always she was eager to do so, and I noticed what use to annoy me about her, was sort of endearing. I could tell she really liked Carter, maybe she had a soft spot for brainiacs. Who was I to judge?

"No, their blood was a weird dark green color wasn't it?" Taya corrected Carter on the fact.

"Yeah, you're right. It looked like a thick sludge. Write that down Taya, oh, and don't forget that they did start to retreat, so that shows signs of fear."

"Got it."

"There were about two feet tall, covered in that nasty scaly skin… hmm what else?"

Taya sat scribbling away before sticking the pencil in her mouth while she tried to remember other details.

They went back and forth like that for what seemed like hours. Max and I sat silently in the back seat, each of us slowly inching closer together until our thighs were touching intimately and I was resting my head on his shoulder staring out the window.

"Hey look! It's Salt Lake." I pointed out the window to the wide expanse of still blue water. "We are almost half way now right?"

"Uh…yea. You two got the map back there? I think we are going to have to change interstates here at some point."

Max and I deciphered the map while Carter steadily made his way through the streets. We had to get off the interstate as it was taking too long to weave through the overabundance of abandoned and wrecked vehicles.

As we drove along, I couldn't help but notice how the city still retained a small morsel of its beauty even after such a cataclysmic event. I admired the architecture in the buildings of the once bustling downtown metropolis and wondered if the city would ever be the same again. Would any city ever be the same again? Would we be able to do everything that Carter said we would? Could we really help give the answer to stop what could very well be the end of humanity? Questions continued to rattle through my head as we drove down the tree-lined city streets.

We stopped for lunch and to refuel after having made it farther south into Utah. This time Max had to siphon the gas and as I watched him fight the urge to vomit, I quietly prayed he would brush his teeth before trying to kiss me again. And then I wondered if we even had any toothpaste.

"I vote that getting the gas remains the guy's job," Taya said as she watched Max leaning over the side of the road with his hands on his knees. His face had contorted into the oddest expressions as he fought his body's revulsion to the taste of gasoline in his mouth. I started to wonder if he had accidently swallowed any.

I placed a hand on his back in a small effort to give comfort and I nodded my head at Taya, "You have a point. I second that."

"Nice try you two," Max said as regained his composure.

Taya stuck her tongue out and leaned against the back of the Bronco next to Carter who was rummaging through the bags.

"Hey dude, can you get me a shirt?" Max asked as he pulled his off and used it to wipe his face.

I couldn't help but stare as his hard stomach was revealed when he tugged at his shirt, and tried not to look too disappointed when he kept his undershirt on. He gave me a side long glance and covered himself in mock embarrassment as Carter chucked a clean - well cleaner - shirt at him, hitting him square in the face. Taya and Carter laughed as they walked to the front of the car.

"Those two are getting awfully chummy," Max said.

"Yeah…they are kind of an odd match, but they sort of even each other out don't you think?"

Max just shrugged and shut the back of the Bronco as he took his turn in the front seat to drive the next leg. "Ok everyone, I want you to keep your arms and legs in the ride at all times. Please remain seated and refrain from using flash photography. Seat belts must be latched securely."

We all laughed and said, "Shut up Max" in unison. He smiled over at me with an extra large grin as I clicked my seat belt closed.

"How is your leg feeling?" I asked him as he started driving.

"It's a lot better, a little sore but I hardly notice it

anymore. What about your shoulder?"

"About the same. I almost can't believe we are half way, I feel like I need to pinch myself. This is all almost over. Well, this part of it at least," I said with a relaxing exhalation.

"I'll pinch you if you'd like." Max gave me a crooked smile and all I could do was blush back at him. His strong hands gripped the steering wheel as he drove and I admired them. It was an odd feeling to find a pair of hands to be so beautiful but it was who they belonged to that mattered to me.

When I broke myself away from staring at Max, I could see Carter's reflection in the side view mirror as he gazed out the window. He looked hopeful, but darkness remained hidden just under the surface. An uncertainty that would remain until we made it to New Mexico and knew for sure if we had made the biggest mistake of our lives. I knew my brother well and he wouldn't be completely happy until we made it to New Mexico. As happy as it had made us all to hear that transmission, I knew Carter was still not one hundred percent convinced.

"Honestly..." Taya broke the silence as she loudly flipped through the pages of Carter's book, "we have some really good information in this thing. I've read it front to back now, a few times, and its slowly building and building. Just think of this combined with what the *U.S. Military* has. They must already know tons of things about them, that's probably why they are doing so well down there. They are building a strong resistance and soon we will be able to kill all the demons and this will be finally over."

Carter looked to her and smiled as she handed him the book. "Thanks. Sometimes I want so badly to have so much knowledge to put into this thing, but other times I want the opposite, because the more we have it in, the more evil there is out there to fill it."

"Well, we won't have to worry about that much longer man. We will be in New Mexico soon." Max added.

We had such bad luck at the beginning of our journey through what was left of civilization, and light was finally starting to show on the horizon, but I couldn't help wondering if there were still unforeseen dangers ahead of us. Always the pessimist I tried to quickly remove those thoughts from my mind as I did not want them entering the universe. If I were able to find some wood to knock on at that moment I would have done it for good measure.

The sky seemed to quickly fade to a warm crimson as the sun set on us. To pass the time and keep our minds off of things, Max and I debated over high school politics. He seemed to think our high school football team would have made it to the state championships and I didn't think they had a chance. Not because I really believed it, but just because it was the opposite of what Max thought and we loved harassing each other.

Taya would chime in commenting that her school *always* won state, Carter on the other hand didn't like football and tried to convince us all, that track and field was a man's true test of endurance and athleticism. Which only fueled Max to demand Carter name one track and field star that was as famous as any football player. When Taya blurted out the name of Bruce Jenner, we all rolled with laughter to her dismay.

"What's so funny? I saw it on that show, *The Kardashians*. He was a track star, he was in the Olympics too."

As we wiped tears of laughter from our eyes, Taya folded her arms in a pout as she stared out the window.

"Hey! Look at that!" She said as she tapped her fingernail on the glass of the window. "Does that flag say something?"

Max slowed the Bronco down to a crawl as we all squinted trying to read the flag as it rippled in the windy sky.

"I think it says safe," Carter said almost as a question. "Stop for a minute Max. Geez, it does say safe."

"What do you think it means?" Taya asked.

For an instant I had thought it was an incredibly dumb question, but then I caught on. Was it a trap? I watched Max as he put the Bronco in park. He slowly stepped out, but left the keys in the ignition. The wind tugged at his flannel shirt and sent his dark hair flying around on his head as he walked away from the Bronco.

"What do you see?" I shouted out to him as he stood holding his hand up to his brow shading his eyes from the last of the setting sun.

"We're not going to go check it out are we?" Taya asked her voice sounding weary. We all stared at each other in silence for a good long moment. "You are all nuts!" Taya shouted. "We are halfway there, lets just keep going."

Carter put his hand on her shoulder. "Taya, you know we have to at least check it out. What if there are people there who need help or people who can help us? Can you live with just driving by, knowing you never even tried? Think of us just driving by you, as you were trapped in that van?"

Taya sighed and stared at her fingers as she knotted the strings hanging from a hole in her frayed jeans. "Fine, but for the record I think this is a really dumb idea."

I watched Taya slide out of the Bronco and stand next to Max at the edge of the road. "Are you sure about this?" I asked Carter.

"Yeah. I've realized that I have been so

consumed with either getting information into this book or just getting to New Mexico, I haven't been thinking about what it is going to take to do those things. I meant what I said to her. I don't think I could live with myself either, knowing that I may have left someone behind. I know you all think I don't care, but I do. This is just a lot to deal with, and as childish as it sounds, I wish Dad was here."

I blinked away the urge to cry and reached over to the back seat to hug my brother. "We don't think you don't care Carter. I know you have a lot of responsibility to bear, and I miss Dad too. You're not alone though, you've got me and Max and Taya too. We will always stand with you, even when you act like a crazed dictator."

A small laughed escaped him. "You're such a brat." He teased.

"Yeah, I know. But you love me anyway."

I jumped out of the Bronco and headed straight to the one other thing that would give me comfort, my shotgun. The familiar weight of it felt right as I placed it over my shoulder. My wound was still tender, but bearable. Strapping the knife to my leg, I walked over to my brother's side and surveyed the white flag billowing in the distance with the words "SAFE" written in red letters on it.

We all hopped back into the Bronco and got off the highway, heading into the town. It was a small town with unique "Mom and Pop" stores lining the trash filled streets. Display windows were smashed everywhere making the sidewalks look like they sparkled in the evening suns soft rays.

"I don't think I have ever seen those words look not so safe ever before in my whole life." Taya whined as we made our way at a snail's pace toward the building.

It appeared to be the town's City Hall building, with a newly, yet haphazardly, built chain link fence lining the property.

"Well… demons wouldn't put up a fence, so there has to be people inside. Right?" Carter asked trying to sound hopeful.

As we came to a stop about fifty feet from the fence, we all slowly crept out of the Bronco, securing our weapons and preparing for anything to leap out at us. I could see Max sniffing the air as he made his way to the front of the Bronco.

"I can't smell anything. Can you?" Max asked.

"No. That's a good sign, so we know at least that there are no hounds nearby." Carter made his way to an entrance of the fence and looked out toward the front of the building.

"How do you suppose we get in?" I asked as I grabbed the links of the fence with my fingers, giving it a tug. The metal felt cold under my fingers and I quickly let go.

"Well, now we know it's not an electric fence." Max added as he approached and I rolled my eyes at him.

The four of us stood along the border of the fence and stared at the imposing building. Its windows had been boarded up and the red brick gave it an ominous look in comparison to the four pale white pillars that stood towering over the entrance.

The wooden front doors suddenly swung open and three men appeared, one taking long strides toward us. He was quickly followed by another man, who stood protectively near the first man. We all stood frozen in place, watching each other until the first man handed his shotgun to the other and walked briskly to the fence.

"What should we do?" Max asked in a quick whisper to Carter as the man approached.

"I'll talk," Carter said quickly and we all steadied ourselves as the man crossed his arms and glowered at us from the other side of the fence. He was wearing camo pants, but not the kind used by the military, they looked like something a hunter would wear. I stared at his boots that looked to be covered in some dried dark substance. Mud perhaps or dirt. I immediately didn't like this man even before he spoke; there was just something about him that made the hairs on the back of my neck stand on end.

"Well, well, what do we have here?"

His voice was nasally and cocky and I didn't like it. "It's just a bunch of kids, Jerry." He shouted back at the man behind him and I leaned to have a better look. He didn't look like a Jerry to me. "Where you kids from?"

"Washington." Carter answered firmly and I was proud to hear the steadiness in his voice.

"Wow. I'm impressed. That's quite a ways to be traveling." His eyes seemed to be inspecting us, giving me the urge to cover myself and Taya, even though I knew he didn't have x-ray vision. "And you seem to have made it all that way no problem at all."

"We've had our share of *obstacles,"* Max added with a bit of irritation in his voice.

"Jerry! Roger! Let those poor kids in already!"

An older man stood just outside the doorway waving his hand in the air. The man closest to us, apparently Roger, gave a heavy sigh and started to pull keys out of his pocket to open the gate.

"Damn it John, I haven't even questioned them yet. We can't let just anybody in here."

We all hesitated after Roger opened the gate and swept his arm across as an invitation to enter. "Ya'll gonna come in or what? I don't want to stand here all damn day."

Carter and Max took the lead as I walked closely behind with Taya in tow. The sound of Roger slamming the gate shut behind us and locking it made us all stop and look back.

"Come on then," John called from the entry way. "Come inside." His voice was so friendly I almost felt that we were in a trance, being lured in by him. The main doors of the building led into a giant foyer that had once greeted important city officials but was now home to, who knew what. John led us quickly down to the end of the hall into a large conference room that had been turned into a dining hall/armory.

"Have a seat, you kids sure look tired." John pulled a chair for himself and sat down with a thud. The sounds of Roger and Jerry placing their weapons back onto a shelf made it a lot easier to relax, so we each took a seat. I looked over to Max and Carter, noting that both of them looked ready to pounce at any second. The edge in the air gave me the urge to pull my shotgun off my back and hold it at the ready.

"Dang, you kids sure are skittish," he commented as he eyed us. "My name is John. You've met Roger and Jerry. Welcome to City Hall. Aren't you going to tell me your names?"

"I'm Carter and he's Max." Taya and I didn't say anything. John looked at us for a moment and then went on.

"Alright then, I don't know what those two meat heads did to freak you kids out, but don't worry about them. They are all bark and no bite." The two cursed under their breath as they left the room and John just waved them off. "I take it you kids saw that flag?"

"Yeah. So, what's the deal here?" Carter asked.

"Well, Carter..." John said the name as if checking that he remembered it correctly, "we have ourselves a little safe house, or more like safe building I guess. We've been here going on a few months now. We've got food, water and weapons, obviously. You kids are welcome to stay of course, but we all pitch in around here so don't think this is a free ride."

"Is it just the three of you?" Taya blurted out.

John chuckled. "No, I think there are about twelve of us now. My wife actually does all the cooking. We've also got a couple kids around your age I think. It's tough, but we get buy. Those damn monsters don't dare come around here anymore. Just a few nights ago we gave them a good ass kicking."

"They're demons," Carter said matter-of-factly, like he needed to correct the guy.

"Hell, I know that. Everybody knows that, but monsters just sounds less, well less damning to me. You sound like that damn Norah lady, all her preaching and what not." It was obvious he was getting worked up about it, but he took a deep breath trying to calm himself down. I caught the expression on Carter's face and could tell he very much wanted to talk to this Norah lady.

"Alright well, I guess I will show you around. Uh, you kids can put those weapons away, ain't nobody here gonna hurt you." None of us made an attempt to remove our weapons, so John just shrugged and started to walk. There was no way any of us were going to leave our weapons, not yet at least. John was right we were skittish.

We followed John around as he showed us the living areas. People had taken over former offices and turned them into decent sleeping areas. We met John's wife in the kitchen. She was preparing a large pot of soup with a few other people who were washing clothes in large metal buckets. The aroma was intoxicating and I had almost forgotten what a real home-cooked meal smelled like. The last time I remember eating something that smelled that good was when my Dad was still alive. The thought of him quickly removed the hint of a smile that had crept on my face.

"Nice to meet you all," John's wife Judy said while stirring the contents of a large stock pot. She quickly wiped her hands on a towel and held out a hand in greeting. She was a tall frail looking lady. She had a friendly demeanor, but there was a sadness about her, which would probably be a common characteristic of anyone we would meet from now on. I thought for a moment that we probably appeared the same way.

Our tour then led us to a small courtyard area where young teen aged kids played hacky sack under the watchful eye of a girl that looked to be about my age. She was pinning clothes up on a line to dry. John introduced her as Norah and she kindly tilted her head at us. She had long red hair that was wrapped up into a frizzy braid. Her freckled face hinted at a former beauty, but the obvious lack of food made her cheek bones stand out. I wondered what she looked like before everything happened and imagined how much prettier she must have been with a full round face.

"This is Norah. She helps maintain this garden here, I'm sure she could use some extra hands if one of you four is willing," John said rather quickly, obviously not wanting the introduction with Norah to last for very long.

"Hello everyone. I'd always accept some extra help."

It was apparent how exhausted she was as she propped the empty laundry basket onto her boney hip and called out for the kids to follow her inside. They obediently followed her orders, and just before Norah slipped into the kitchen Carter announced that he would help her. I felt Taya stir next to me and was sure she didn't much like the idea of the two of them spending time together.

Norah nodded with a slight smile, which I would later discover irritated Taya immensely.

"That's nice of you Carter, but that's mainly a

woman's job around here." John commented.

I wasn't sure if that statement offended Carter or not.

"I don't mind. I've been known for having a green thumb," Carter said. I then realized that he really wanted to an opportunity to talk to Norah and get her opinion on what was going on. It usually was the case that the person that seemed to not fit in with the crowd was the one who knew the most.

"He could probably do wonders for your zucchini plants over there." I added to make Carter's claim more convincing.

John eyed us suspiciously for a moment and then directed us back into the building, leading us to our room. A woman quickly retreated upon our entry after having added an extra cot for us to sleep on.

"Alright, this can be your room. We don't have much, but we have plenty of blankets and…looks like Sherry brought you some towels and soap, so you could clean yourselves up."

"Oh my gosh a shower!" Taya squealed as she ran to snatch the bar of soap off a nearby table.

John smiled at her childlike antics and then continued. "I believe dinner will be in about thirty minutes, so there is time for you all to get cleaned up. Alright then, I'll let you get to it." He left the room closing the door behind him.

"Do you guys remember where the bathrooms were?" Taya asked already with soap and towels in tow.

"Just hold on Taya, I don't think any of us should be going anywhere alone," Carter said.

"I am just going to shower, what's the big deal?"

"We don't know these people very well yet. Listen, I'll go with you ok?" I said.

Carter silently mouthed the words thank you as we left the room. I had to admit to myself I was rather excited about the idea of a shower. I was sweaty and tired from the long day of driving and I wanted to wash away the stresses of the day. However, what awaited us in the bathroom was far from what we had expected.

Chapter 9

Of course, a city hall building wasn't going to have a proper shower. It appeared that they had turned the handicap stall into a makeshift shower. The toilet had been removed and a hole had been made into the plaster wall to hook a shower head into the water line. We took turns showering, while the other stood guard at the door and I let Taya go first.

"Hey Abby…" Taya called from the shower. "Why do you think Carter wanted to help with the gardening so bad?"

"I think he wants to question that Norah girl. She seems to have a different view point then everyone else here." Taya didn't have a response to that.

"Did you see that door Roger and that other guy were guarding?" She asked.

"Yeah, that I was a little curious about. I can't image what they could possibly need to guard like that." During our tour we had walked down a hallway that had a large security door bolted into the frame. The two men who had "greeted" us at the front gate guarded it and when Max asked what they were doing John wouldn't answer. John said it was private business and we need not worry ourselves about it, which only made us more concerned.

"Maybe they have supplies they don't want anyone to steal."

"No, that can't be it. Besides if someone were going to steal they wouldn't get very far would they?"

"No, I guess your right."

I thought more about what could be behind that door, while Taya finished her shower leaving me very little warm water. The water quickly turned cold, but it still felt good to be clean. I quickly ripped the bandage off my shoulder, and tried to gently rub soap on the wound. It looked better than it felt. After getting as clean as I could and wrapping myself in a towel I walked carefully out of the stall across the slippery tile floor, only to find that Taya had left me alone. I should have known it was getting too quiet.

I cursed her under my breath and quickly got dressed. Rummaging through my bag on the floor I found a brush and got to work on my hair until I was able to put it into a proper ponytail. I stared at my reflection in the mirror for a moment and found that I did look a bit better, not so sleep deprived or zombie-like, even though I still felt like it.

Walking out of the bathroom with bag in tow I ran right into Roger. "Oh sorry." He leered at me and I got this sneaking suspicion that he had been lurking around and worried if he had been in the bathroom with me without me even knowing it. I quickly retreated and found our room, shutting the door firmly before resting my back against it.

"These people are fucking creepy," I said.

"I'll agree with you on that," Max said, startling me.

I considered telling him about Roger hanging around outside the bathroom, but I knew Max would go ape-shit and probably cause a very unwanted scene.

"They are hiding something, I just don't know what."

"I've been thinking the same thing. There is just something about this place that makes my hair stand on end."

Max nodded and took a seat down next to me. Seeing my wound visibly under the strap of my tank top, he sighed loudly.

"Abs, you should keep that thing covered. At least until it heals a little more," Max quickly bandaged up my shoulder and topped it off with a kiss for good measure.

"Max, I don't wanna stay here for very long."

"We won't. We should stay here for the night at the very least and leave first thing in the morning. I know Carter will agree with that. If he wants to get information from that Norah girl, he is going to have to work fast."

Max and I embraced each other before heading to the dining hall, for what we both were certain would be a very interesting dinner.

Carter had managed to seat himself right next to Norah, and she politely nodded at Max and me as we walked in. Taya on the other hand, sat on the other side of Carter with a scowl firmly affixed to her face.

Max and I took seats across from them and although everyone seemed to be in cheerful moods, I still felt like everyone was watching us. My grip on Max's hand tightened as John rose from his seat to announce our arrival and welcome us. There were new faces that I had not remembered seeing while on the tour, but they looked friendly enough. I just couldn't help but notice that no one seemed to want to make eye contact with John. Did they seem to shrink back whenever he spoke to someone, or was I just being paranoid?

"Quiet down everyone. I would like you all to welcome the newcomers to our group, to our family. I know I speak for all of you when I say that we are happy to have you stay with us. These are dark times and we all must stick together to find the light. We must all be willing to work together to find whatever small bits of peace are left in the world. So let us raise our glasses to this blessing of finding fellow survivors, and new friends." Everyone raised their cups and spoke quiet amens and praises for our safe arrival to them.

"So Carter… Taya tells me you saved her from three of those demon birds. Is this true?" John said.

"Uh…yeah." We were all a little confused as to when Taya was able to tell him anything. "We all saved her. We didn't do anything that anybody else wouldn't have done."

"Very true, boy. That is my very point. We must be willing to risk anything to destroy these demons. To save any lasting pieces of humanity we have. That is a very difficult lesson for some people to learn. Even with the state the world is in, not everyone is willing to help those in need."

A dribble of drool started to roll down John's chin and he wiped it off with the back of his hand and continued. "I hear you also have yourself a dictionary of some sort? With information about these...demons?

We all shot Taya a penetrating glance, as Carter recovered. "Yes, I have been cataloging information about the demons."

The room broke out in sudden chatter as people expressed their shock and fear. "Only to discover their weaknesses. To defeat them, we must understand them."

The people calmed down at this and John raised his hand to calm everyone down. I was quickly discovering that John was the ringleader of this group of survivors, but it seemed so much like people were afraid of him. His voice was kind and welcoming, but there was something crazy in his eyes

"Great minds think a like then. You must have some very valuable information to have made it so far. Later tonight, you and I will talk. I'm sure we could learn a great deal from each other."

Carter agreed and everyone went on with their own conversations. John walked from table to table, in what would have looked to be a courteous host, but appeared more to be an act of a watchful guard dog.

"Abby..." Max whispered into my ear as we

finished eating. "I'm going to go with Carter tonight, keep an eye on him. Can you watch Taya?"

"I don't need a babysitter," Taya spat almost too loudly.

"I didn't say you did, now ssh! I want you two girls to stick together tonight. This dude is freaking me out, he's got some cult going on here, or something, and I don't want us to have any part in it. Some of these people seem genuinely afraid of him and his two goons, and I am not even sure that Judy lady is his wife. Just look at her, she is frozen stiff. She won't even look at him."

I looked over at her and he was right. Judy was sitting, sunken into her seat, obviously trying to make herself invisible. Her eyes were red and puffy and as she reached to clean up John's dishes I noticed something stick out underneath her shirt sleeve.

"Did you see that?" I asked Max and Taya.

"Yea, it looked like a bandage." Max answered. "They are around her wrists, you don't think…?"

"Maybe… a lot of people can't handle it, or would rather do it themselves than wait for a demon to kill them and do who knows what with their body."

"What are you two whispering about?" Taya asked, obviously not catching on.

"Judy, she has bandages on her wrists."

"John says she is depressed. They lost their son during the last attack."

"How do you know that?" I tried to shout and whisper at her at the same time.

"John told me. I ran into him walking back to our room after showering. He asked me some questions. Look you two, he seems nice." She pleaded.

"You mean when you ditched me while I was showering? You were suppose to watch the door while I was in there Taya."

"Sorry. I wanted to talk to Carter before he got in here for dinner."

"Thanks a lot, you left me there for sausage neck over there to snoop on." I almost pointed my finger at Roger, but quickly retracted my hand.

"What?" Max questioned raising his voice.

"Don't worry. I'm not certain he did anything, he was just creeping me out."

"Why didn't you tell me Abs?"

"Cause I didn't want you to freak out. Look there goes Carter, why don't you go with him before John catches up with him."

"Fine. Just promise me you are going to be careful."

"I promise."

Max cupped his hand to my face and then quickly but casually left the room after Carter, heading for the courtyard I guessed. I saw Taya's expression looking at where Carter and Norah had just left the room and sighed loudly at her.

"Taya, snap out of it. Now is not the time to be jealous."

"What? I'm not jealous. I know he is just using her for information."

"Whatever, let's go back to the room."

Making our way out of the room and into the hallway I saw out of the corner of my eye Judy sitting alone. She was curled up into an armchair holding a steaming cup of something.

"Judy?"

"Oh, yes, hi dear. Do you need something?" Her eyes were kind and did not hold the faint madness that I found in John's eyes.

"No, um, I just was wondering if you were ok."

"Ok as can be expected." There was awkward silence, but I truly felt sorry for the lady. She had just lost her son and was obviously have great difficulty dealing with her grief.

"See Abby, she's ok," Taya said as she pulled at my hand. I hesitated for a moment, trying to think of something to say but nothing came to mind. Judy just sat there, holding a cup in hand and taking small sips of the steaming liquid.

As we walked back into the hallway, I thought I faintly heard Judy say be careful, but I wasn't certain. When we made it back to the room, I had to listen to a full account of Carter's conversation with Norah and how Taya didn't think Norah was pretty at all.

"I mean she dresses like a total prude. Did you see that shirt she was wearing? It's the middle of summer!"

I wasn't really listening, but tried to time my

mhm's and *uhuh's* at the correct time until she eventually talked herself to sleep. To pass the time I packed up all of our bags and even stole the bars of soap John had given us for good measure. Then I sat on the floor by my cot and cleaned my shotgun. Realizing that the last time I had done it was before we left home. The familiar procedure was therapeutic and brought back memories of my father teaching me. He taught me how to shoot, how to aim, and even timed me on my speed for assembly.

    Even though Taya was in the room with me, sleeping in her cot, I felt utterly alone as hot tears burned my eyes. Every burning drop that I had been holding back, came pouring out and I silently wept while reassembling my shotgun.

    When the water works had finally stopped and I regained control of my emotions, it was pretty much impossible to sleep. I looked at my watch and it was almost one in the morning and neither of the guys were back yet. I tried to be patient and decided I would try the small radio that Charlie had given me. I pulled it out of my bag and turned it on only to hear static on every station. Feeling frustrated and afraid for the guys I fought the urge to throw something against the wall.

I was really starting to get worried and wanted to go look for them, but I didn't want to leave Taya alone, so I decided to wake her. I crossed the room to where she was sleeping, and shook her shoulder, probably a little harder than I had meant to, but I was anxious and worried.

"Taya you gotta wake up."

"What? Why, what's going on?" Her lids were still heavy over her eyes and dark streaks ran down her face. I guess I wasn't the only one, who felt the need to cry that night.

"They aren't back yet. We need to go find them."

"What time is it?"

"Almost one. Carter and Max should have been back ages ok. We need to go."

At the thought of Carter being missing Taya leaped out of bed and sprang into action. She was ready to go even before I was.

"You got everything?" I asked almost out of

breath just from the rush of anxiety that was coursing through me. Taya nodded her head and latched Carter's bag onto her back. I heaped my duffel bag onto mine, it felt awkward but at least it wasn't heavy.

We stepped gingerly out into the dark hallway. It was total darkness except for a faint glow emitting from a room at the end of the hall.

"Wait, Abby." Taya tugged at my arm and pulled me against a wall. "Isn't that the room they were guarding? Maybe we shouldn't go in there, what if they are just outside talking with Norah still?"

I could tell Taya didn't really believe what she was saying, that she was just afraid of what we were going to find in that room.

"Taya, look around you. This place is a crypt, there are no lights anywhere else, except that room. If you are too scared then take this stuff to the Bronco and wait for us there, but I am going in there and getting my brother and Max."

I tried to stay light on my feet as I made my way down the hall. When I got to the door I could hear voices muffled, but not well enough to make anything out. I swallowed my fear and leaned my face onto the crack of the open door. I was expecting another office or room of some sort, but instead it was a lit stairwell, leading down into what must have been a basement. I looked back as the sliver of light from the door illuminated the hallway. I saw Taya still struggling to decide what she was going to do, and then she silently made a quick jog to my side.

"Ok, let's do this."

I thought about it for a moment, and decided we had better leave our bags behind, so we deposited them along the wall just outside the doorway. If we needed to make a quick escape we could grab them on the run. I worried that the door might creek so I opened it just enough so that we could slip in. I took my knife out, even though I favored my shotgun, but I knew we were in close quarters in a basement and I didn't want to risk hurting the guys.

Taya had pulled out the small handgun Carter had given her and when I noticed she still had the safety on, I switched it off and handed her the knife. Her hands trembled and I could tell that as brave as she was trying to be, she was terrified.

We both held our breath as we walked slowly down the first stairwell, making the voices grow slightly louder with each step. At the landing of the second flight of stairs there was another door that was partially ajar. The instant I saw the familiar pattern of Max's blue plaid shirt I bolted down the steps and flew through the doorway with Taya on my heels.

The scene that lay before us was nothing short of terrifying. The room looked to be a makeshift jail. Max and Carter were up against a wall, their faces bloodied and bruised and Norah was laying on the floor weeping. She had a firm grip on a bloody towel that was wrapped around her forearm. A ripple of fear rolled through me as I watched what they were doing. John's two goons Roger and Jerry were standing over her with smiles on their smug faces. Roger grabbed a small bucket near Norah's feet and slid it to the demon that quickly slammed its muzzle into it drinking up whatever was in it.

"Well look what we have here," John said as he smiled at Taya and me.

I quickly shoved the handgun into my pants and pulled my shotgun from off my back and cocked it. "Yes, what do we have here?" I asked with complete disgust in my voice.

"Abby, Taya, get out of here!" Max shouted. I saw Carter look up and realized he hadn't seen us come in because one of his eyes were swollen shut. Blood was smeared over both their faces and the sight of them made a tidal wave of rage flow through me.

"No, I think they'll be staying," John said as he took two steps toward us and that's when I saw it. As John walked toward us I could clearly see what was locked behind the bars in the cell behind him. It was a giant demon, much like the one that Taya's mother had hit with her car.

Chapter 10

It was twice as big as any hound we had ever seen. It looked like a giant wolf and its black eyes bore into my soul. The sight of it terrified me and it took a moment for me to force my eyes to look away. Crimson blood dripped from its muzzle as it snarled at Roger and Jerry who stood nearby. The demon limped around in its cage. One of its legs appeared to be broken, but the creature continued to put its full weight down with every step, sending the echo of bones cracking with every movement.

"You look confused," John said sounding like the situation was completely normal. "I thought your brother would understand what we are doing here, but obviously he was not as enlightened as I thought he was." John waved his gun around and I saw Max put his arm protectively over Carter. I wanted to run to them and find out what happened, but I couldn't. I needed to think of something clever and quick to get us out of this.

"Well, why don't you enlighten *me* then?" I said as I took a step further into the room not taking my aim off of John.

"Well, my dear, frankly it's quite uncomfortable to talk with a gun pointed at me, why don't you put that away, so we can be more civilized."

"Not a chance."

John then nodded over to Roger and Jerry who both pulled out their guns, each pointing one at Taya and me and the other at Max and Carter.

"You see, we desire the same thing, do we not? We all want to rid the world of these demons, do we not? As you can see, we have this specimen here. He's quite resilient, damn thing won't tell us what we want to know."

"What is there to know? Just kill it and be done with it?"

"Ahh, but we don't want to kill it. If we do that we can't figure out its weaknesses."

The demon growled and slammed its giant claw against the bars of the cage and John laughed at it. Taya stifled a scream as the demon's growl echoed off the cement walls.

"I think you're pissing it off," I said as I looked down at Norah who was still cowering at Roger's feet. "What did you do to her?"

"Nothing that I haven't done to myself or anyone else here for that matter. We all have sacrifices to make, and it was her turn."

"Go! Just get out of here!" Carter shouted this time as blood trickled out of a split lip. Jerry took two quick strides and punched him sending Carter falling to the floor.

"What the hell, jerk! He didn't do anything!" Max grabbed Carter's body from off the floor and helped him stand up. I wanted to start crying, but I had to be strong. I thought back on something my father had told me once and tried to collect the strength and courage to do what I knew I needed to do. It was up to me to save them and I had to be willing to do anything to accomplish that. I swallowed back the lump in my throat and steadied my feet as I prepared myself.

Lowering the hand that held the shotgun I pulled the gun out of my waistband, aiming and pulling the trigger in one fell sweep. The bullet tore through the side of Jerry's head and he staggered only for an instant before falling to the floor. His body landed against the cage bars and the demon quickly slid its massive arm to thrash at Jerry's lifeless body.

"Maybe I was wrong about you," John said sounding slightly amused.

"Max you and Carter get over here now!" I shouted as I held my shotgun and handgun pointed at the two remaining men. I wasn't sure if I could fire them both of them at the same time, but I sure as hell wasn't afraid to try.

Taya who had remained silent during the whole scene quickly grabbed the handgun from me then ran to help Max get Carter as he struggled to find his footing. Taya slid under Carter's body and guided him out of the room. Somehow her scrawny figure had found the strength to carry his near dead weight out the room and up the stairs.

Max stayed behind with me and his presence by my side filled me with strength.

"Let her go," I said as calmly but as sternly as I could, trying to enunciate each word firmly.

"She can leave, she paid her dues for now." Roger yanked her hair and Norah screamed in pain as her head was thrust upward.

"You people have lost your freaking minds!"

"Why is that? Because we feel that each of our lives are worth losing to gain the greater good? If you could save everyone, just by killing her, you wouldn't do that?" John pointed to me and Max shook his head.

"No, I wouldn't. What you people are doing is wrong and you know it. You really think you can keep that thing here, torturing it and feeding it to keep it alive and not have to pay the consequences? These are friggin' demons from hell, you really think that anything you can do to it will compare to what it went through in hell?" Max shouted.

John's expression faltered for a moment, but he quickly regained his composure. "Boy, you have no idea of what we have already learned." Just then the demon thrust its arm between the bars catching Roger on his shoulder and pulled him firmly against the bars. Roger's screams were quickly halted when the demon stuck its long snout out and clamped down firmly on Roger's skull.

John whirled and started unloading his gun into the demon as well as into what was left of Roger and I knew this was our chance. Max and I bolted for Norah. He scooped her up and we ran for the stairs. John was cursing as he ran out of bullets and he quickly snagged Roger's gun that lay on the cold cement floor. As we made our way to the top of the stairs I heard the loud clatter of the metal bars clang against the concrete.

"Shit! Run, go, go, go!"

We leapt into the hallway and I quickly slammed the door shut behind us, then I pushed a nearby couch in front of it. "That's not going to hold it for long," Max said as we ran down the hallway, Norah bouncing in his arms. I realized I didn't grab my bag and halted.

"Abby what are you doing? Let's go!"

"I forgot my bag, keep going I'll be right there!"

"What? Are you serious, forget the damn bag let's go!"

Max turned and ran for the front door, but I quickly ran back for my bag anyway. I found it and slung it over my shoulder as I heard a pounding coming from the basement door. The demon had finished its work on John and now it was after us. I felt a sudden surge of panic as I thought about the other people in the building. Like we were somehow responsible for letting it lose on them, but there was nothing we could do, it was too late.

As I neared the front door, I saw the familiar lights of the Bronco in the distance. Taya had somehow managed to drive through the front gate and was already loading Max and Norah into the back seat. I saw Max look up after me, but as I reached the doors something caught my attention from the corner of my eye. It was Judy. She was running out of a room with four other people in tow.

"Please, take them!" She pleaded.

I wasn't sure how we could all fit in the Bronco, but I couldn't say no.

"Let's go!" I shouted as I ushered them out and we ran across the front lawn. The night had grown cold and my lungs burned as we sprinted toward the Bronco. The sound of the demon growling tore through the night air and seemed to echo off the buildings. It stood at the doorway only long enough to survey its prey and then leaped onto the lawn like a lion.

It quickly fell upon the two people in the rear. Without missing a beat the demon, leapt onto a third person as they stumbled in their attempt to flee. In one swift stroke it slit the woman's throat with its long claws.

As we made it to the Bronco, I jumped onto the step by the passenger side door and Max held onto Judy and the last person as they clung to the back of the vehicle.

"Go!" I shouted as Taya put the Bronco into gear and sped out of the lawn, sending bits of grass and soil flying in our wake. It took some quick maneuvering but Taya barreled down the main road successfully and flew onto the highway as the demon chased after us howling, falling farther and farther behind. I crawled in through the window, as Max helped the two women into the back of the Bronco. We didn't want to risk stopping. The Bronco lurched and screeched loudly as Taya struggled to change gears.

"Here I got it." I slid Taya over while holding the wheel and took over the driver's seat.

Taya quickly went to Carter, surveying his wounds. "What happened back there?" No one answered.

Carter made a groaning sound and I tried to look at him through the rear view mirror. My heart was hammering in my chest and as badly as I wanted to stop the Bronco and crawl into the back to look at him, I kept my foot on the gas and pushed forward.

"Here." Max handed Taya our first aid kit as he crawled from the back seat into the passenger seat next to me. I could feel his eyes on me and I wanted to look at him so badly, but I knew if I did I would burst into tears and completely lose any sense of self-control that I was so desperately clinging to.

Max silently rested his hand on my thigh and my chest heaved as tears burned my cheeks. Taya managed to clean up Carter's face, making it look considerably better. It was still swollen and bruised, but with the absence of blood he looked similar to that of what a professional boxer would after a fight.

Somehow, Taya had managed to crush up some Ibuprofen into some water and was attempting to get Carter to swallow it. As it dribbled down his split lip she quickly wiped it off gently and squeezed his hand. Pushing herself up against the side of the Bronco, she wadded a shirt into a ball and placed Carter's head up against her. It looked as though he fell asleep instantly as Taya whispered at him. I felt an instant sense of gratitude for this girl, who we barely knew. Seeing her take such good care of my brother made my heart ache and as I saw her tightly hold onto his hand I knew with finality the love she had for him.

Judy, Norah and the other young lady we had managed to save sat silently in the back amongst our bags, their faces frozen in fear and anguish. The girl I did not recognize buried her head into Judy's chest as Judy slowly ran her fingers through the girl's hair. Norah sat with her face staring out behind us, her expression portraying that she was very far away from her body. I tried not to think about all the people we had left behind. I knew there was no way we could have saved everyone, but deep down I still felt guilt over it.

    Images of the scene in the basement kept flashing through my mind. The sight of the demon mauling Jerry and then Roger made my stomach lurch and my body started to protest even more when the sound of the bullet hitting Jerry's skull played out in my head. The bullet I aimed at him, killed him. My logical mind told me there was no other way, that in the end someone was going to die down there and if I didn't do what I did, it could have been any of us, but my heart screamed at me. In a war with demons, I took another person's life. Could I live with the choice I made?

    After what felt like an eternal battle inside my mind I swallowed the lump that was building in my throat and with one deep breath I found my resolve. I could live with what I did; I had to because I knew without a doubt that I would not be able to live without Max, my brother or even Taya. They were my family now, and no matter how afraid I was, I would do anything I could to protect them.

"What happened?" I asked after a long while of silence. Even though I knew the details might be difficult to hear, I wanted to know what had occurred and caused them to end up in that basement.

Max looked at me and I saw the fear hiding behind his expression. "I was watching Carter talk to Norah in the courtyard. I kept my distance just watching them and then all of a sudden John's two goons showed up. They started talking to Norah and they got into an argument. Things started to get heated and they tried to drag her off. Carter tried to stop them and that's when they started fighting." Max paused taking deep breaths and I could tell he was trying to keep his anger controlled.

"I thought it was some kind of jealously issue at first, so I wasn't going to intercede. Maybe they didn't want one of their girls talking to us, but from the fear I saw in her eyes, I knew something was wrong. I ran at them and took Jerry to the floor, but Roger quickly knocked Carter out and they both ganged up on me. Before I knew it they were dragging us down those stairs and I saw them throwing Carter into a heap on the floor next to me."

Max looked up at me with tears threatening to fall down his bruised face. I had to quickly look away and focus on the road before me. I had never seen Max cry in all the years I knew him and if I were to see it now, I don't know if I could stand it. He was my pillar of strength and to see him broken would break me as well. I held onto the hand he rested on my thigh and squeezed, trying to pass on what little bit of strength I had left.

It seemed to help as Max took a deep breath, and went on, his voice sounding steadier. "John showed up and was preaching about how we must all make sacrifices to the greater good. That everyone else had paid the price and Norah could not be an exception. Then he pulled out a long knife and quickly sliced her forearm. They let her blood pour into a bucket and gave it to the demon."

My jaw dropped and I looked back at Norah, but her face remained expressionless. "They gave it her blood? But why?"

"John believed that sating the demon's hunger and feeding it our blood, while keeping it alive would somehow give us leverage as a form of bribery for the demon," Judy said woodenly.

"That's flipping nuts." Taya added a little too loudly and Carter stirred in her arms. She quickly shushed him and glared back at Judy.

I looked at Taya warningly and encouraged Judy to go on. "When our son died, something changed in John. After that night, he had this crazy idea in his head that we had to sacrifice ourselves to them. He thought that by doing so, it would appease them and they would leave us alone. We were all required to give the demon a taste of our blood, to see who it most desired as its sacrifice."

I was completely dumbfounded and at a loss for words. What to say to something like that, I wasn't entirely sure.

"What gave him the idea that sacrificing yourselves would work? How is that even part of a normal thought process?" Max asked, clearly not holding back any inflection of disdain.

"Before the demons came, my husband was a professor. He used to study ancient cultures and customs. I believe that he lost all sense of humanity when he saw our son die, and was willing to do anything… he used to be a brilliant man."

"Yeah… really damn brilliant," Taya snapped. Judy looked away obviously ashamed. I probably should have said something to Taya, but she was right. She had the balls to say what I couldn't. It was not Judy's fault that her husband completely snapped and turned into a total nutcase. I remembered then the bandage I had seen on her arm at dinner and realized that she too must have made the sacrifice her husband demanded.

I did not know what it could possibly feel like to lose a child, and the sense of loss that must accompany it, but I did know what I felt when I thought I was going to lose Carter and Max. I would have done anything to save them, and I suppose I did. As much as I tried to fight it, I again relived the moment that I pulled the trigger and shot Jerry in the head. The sound of the bullet hitting his flesh made the hair on my arms stand on end. I had never killed anyone before, we had always focused solely on defending ourselves from the demons, that it had never occurred to me that we would have to defend ourselves from anyone else, but then I remember the sick feeling in my gut when I saw Carter fall to the floor and the crazed look I saw in John's eyes. I realized I would have killed them all if I had to, and that realization made me want to vomit. Was I as bad as they were? If I lost Carter or Max would I turn into John?

"Abby what's wrong? You're shaking." Max asked with a concerned look in his eyes.

I immediately felt deeply sorry for him. He had gone through more that I had and he was more concerned about me, just like he always was. "I am just freaked out Max. That was a really close call. What are we going to do now?"

"We are going to keep going," Carter said startling all of us, his voice sounding hoarse. Taya told him not to speak and when he seemed to fall back to sleep she looked out the window. Her brow wrinkled as she scowled at the landscape, making her look a lot older.

Max sighed and pulled out the map from the glove box. "Where are we exactly?"

"There is a sign coming up," I said.

"Hmm...Shiprock, New Mexico. Well, at least we made it to New Mexico, right?"

I forced a smile for him - he always was such an optimist. He had always tried to lighten the mood through sarcasm or humor. Sometimes it worked, sometimes it didn't but the fact that he always tried was one of the things that made me love him.

"I'm not too good with math, but I would say we are about four hundred miles away."

"Thank God. So, when will we get there? Tonight?" Taya asked sounding eager.

"Maybe. If we don't hit too many big cities that slow us down it is possible."

"Where are we going?" Judy asked from the back of the Bronco.

"New Mexico." Taya answered, as if the question were directed to her. I let her go on with it anyway. She and Carter had grown close and I knew he had probably talked her ear off about all his plans. "There is a military base there that has established a resistance. Haven't you heard any of the transmissions?"

Judy nodded solemnly. "John believed that the transmissions were a ploy used by the demons to lure humans there. He ordered us to destroy all the radios to rid ourselves of the temptation. He said to listen to them was to let the demons into your heart and corrupt your mind with a false sense of safety."

"And you all just destroyed the radios, no questioned asked?" I said.

"Some of us refused, but in the end the radios were destroyed anyway," Norah added flatly.

"Sounds like you were part of some kind of cult." Taya commented. "Why would you stay there?"

"What other choice do we have? What would you have us do? Walk around aimlessly in this warzone, waiting for the next demon to pick us off?"

I could see Taya on the verge of losing her temper; my brother would get the same expression on his face when he got upset. So, I nodded to Max to say something to calm them down.

Max turned in his seat to face everyone. "Listen, it doesn't really matter does it? We are all here now and there is nothing any of us can do about any of that. The only thing any of us needs to worry about is getting to New Mexico and doing everything we can to send all these demons back to where they came from. Now, do you know any of what John learned from that thing while he had it locked up?"

"Not much. It would only speak of one thing, repeating it over and over." Judy said with fear rippling through her voice.

"Wait, who?" I asked shocked of what I thought she just said.

"The demon."

"They talk?" Max blurted what I was thinking.

"Yes, like I said. When it spoke it would say only one thing and one thing only."

"Well, what would it say?" Taya asked sounding as equally shocked as the rest of us.

"John called it the prophecy. The demon said, *"The day has come when God looked unto his creations and wept, for they had forsaken him. In his misery he shall turn from mankind and abandon them to the fate, they so earned. The Devil, Satan, King of Hell, most powerful seeker of souls will open his gates and release his minions unto the land. Then shall there be darkness. Then shall there be pain and misery as the world has never seen. As the enemy of the righteous devours the lost souls of the earth he will take his throne and rule the land for all eternity."*

Judy spoke the words woodenly, but I could sense the fear she was holding back. I quickly looked to Taya who was whispering a prayer to herself. The prophecy that her mother use to tell her, was spoken by a demon. The thought chilled the air around me and I saw Max squeezing his mother's gold cross in his hand so hard his knuckles were white.

"I've heard that before," Taya said softly. "My mother use to tell me that, but I thought she was just superstitious. Even after seeing the demons attacking people I still couldn't believe that such a thing could happen."

I could sense that Taya felt guilty for thinking her mother was crazy. I wanted to say something to comfort her, but couldn't.

We drove onward in silence, stopping only when we had to go to the bathroom and once more for Max to empty out the remaining gas tanks we had, in order to refill the Bronco.

"Do you really think its true Max? That the devil really is on earth?" I asked Max after he relieved me from driving as we headed into Albuquerque.

"As much as it doesn't make sense, it does make sense. I haven't even wrapped my head around it yet I don't think."

"Kind of makes it hard to think that there is a way to beat this, knowing that the Devil himself is out there."

I didn't want to sound like such a downer, but Judy had dropped a pretty damn big bomb on us. One would think that if the world were being devoured by demons, you might mention that you have one locked up in your basement and maybe even throw in the fact that it talks.

"Don't think like that Abs. We will find a way. We've done pretty well so far. With the exception of the last escapade of course, but that wasn't our entire fault. We were on guard against demons; we didn't think we would have to worry about other people attacking us with an apocalypse going on."

Judy looked up for a moment, no doubt she wanted to protest any negative comments about her crazy husband, but she thought better and kept her mouth shut.

I gave Max my best impression of his famous devilish grin and propped my feet up on the dash. The whites of my converse sneakers were scuffed and dirty, so I attempted to give them a good shining with my thumb and some good old-fashioned saliva to help pass the time.

"He's right," Norah said almost to herself. I was going to ask who she was talking about, because so much time had passed since anyone had said anything.

"Of course I am," Max said returning a smile back at me, relishing in the fact that someone admitted he was right and we giggled as we heard Carter moan in protest. Taya then let out a quick laugh, even though it was obvious she tried to prevent it, and Carter gave a weak smile before closing his eyes again.

Making our way through town had been easier than it had been anywhere else. Max attributed it to the fact that we were so close to the military base, and was determined this was a result of so many people making their way to safety. A statement that seemed to perk up Carter quite a bit, making him much more coherent.

"I used to really want to visit New Mexico… before everything happened," Norah said trying to make conversation.

"Why is that?" Taya asked in a tone so friendly it almost surprised me, but I figured spending the last few hours with Carter snuggled up against her put her feelings of jealousy to rest.

"I was really into astronomy, spirituality, and the whole extraterrestrial bit. I wanted to take a trip across the United States one day and visit all the major spots like Area 51, Roswell and Sedona." When no one said anything she started to look embarrassed that she had said anything. Laughing at herself a little she said, "Sounds stupid now though."

"No, it's not stupid. I don't think you're stupid. I was just trying to figure out why you would want to visit Sedona," Taya said.

"Oh, well Sedona is likely one of the most

spiritual locations in the country. It's full of amazing energy vortexes."

Visibly attempting to hold back on her enthusiasm, Norah then gave us a full account of her cross-country journey to any and every popular point of supernatural or paranormal events. I had always found such topics extremely boring, but the passion in her voice had peaked my interest. To hear someone talk about something they cared so much about made me slightly envious. There was nothing I particularly excelled at and nothing that I felt I was that passionate about. I mean there were a lot of things I enjoyed, but nothing that I would drive across country to go after.

"Shit!" Max exclaimed slamming his hands on the steering wheel as the Bronco shuddered to a halt.

"What happened?" He'd startled me as well as everyone else in the Bronco and we all took on expressions of instant panic. Max jumped out of the Bronco as clouds of white smoke starting seeping out from under the hood.

Taya started panicking first, repeating "Oh my God" over and over, while the younger girl that Judy had been mothering started bawling. Carter attempted to get out to help find out what was wrong, but he wouldn't be any help with one eye nearly swollen shut, so I ordered him to stay while I jumped out. Then I thought that even if Carter's eye wasn't swollen he probably wouldn't be able to help much anyway, the boy didn't know a thing about cars. In fact, he knew even less than I did which wasn't much at all.

The stifling heat of the late afternoon sun hit me hard and I quickly yanked my hair into a ponytail as I rounded the front of the Bronco. Max had the hood up and was using his shirt to attempt to open the valve to the radiator.

"Damn this thing is hot."

"What do you think is wrong with it?"

"What happened?" Taya called from inside the Bronco.

"Just sit tight!" Max called out to her. "Abby I need you to get back in the Bronco and keep everyone calm, ok? Can you do that for me?"

The concern in his voice made me worry. "Yeah, okay." I turned to walk away and looked back at him.

"Can you fix it?"

Max didn't say a word cause the expression on his face said it all, we were doomed.

"What's wrong with the engine?" Carter asked immediately as I got back in the car. The coolness from the air conditioner was already starting to dissipate.

"Max is taking a look at it. So, how are you feeling?" I asked trying to change the subject.

"I feel like I got my ass kicked. Now tell me what's wrong with the Bronco." Carter's short temper was starting to flare up and I knew he wasn't going to drop it until I told him what he wanted to know. I thought briefly for a moment on how I thought he would probably make a perfect cop. He was always so pushy and cocky, just like every cop I had ever met.

"It doesn't look good," I said, trying to speak it in a whisper because I didn't want everyone to panic, but it was futile. Even whispers aren't quiet enough when everyone is confined in one vehicle like a bunch of sardines.

I heard Judy take a deep breath and then she opened the trunk door in one smooth movement. "We will have to walk the rest of the way then."

"What? Are you crazy?" Taya asked flipping around in the back seat to face her.

"What other choice do we have?"

Taya growled in frustration and turned around to kick the back of the empty driver's seat like a child having a temper tantrum.

"Ok. Everybody calm down for a second. Abby where are we?" Carter asked.

"Umm..." I frantically grabbed the map attempting not to rip it and stared at it trying to remember the name of the city we had just driven through. "We just left Las Cruces not too long ago. It's about another fifty miles or so to the military base."

"Fifty miles, ok we can do that." Carter clapped his hands. "Ok, everyone pack only what you can carry and make it quick we need to move out."

I helped Judy pack up what we had left of our food and water into one bag, while Taya rushed to every nearby car hoping to find one that would start. When she eventually gave up she resigned herself to trying to make some sort of umbrella using car antennae's and some kind of wind breaker jacket she ripped up to block the sun.

I found Max standing alone about twenty feet from the Bronco with his back to me. His arms were crossed and he was staring intently at the imposing mountain side lining the distant city of Las Cruces. We didn't speak at first. We just stood next to each other in a comfortable silence.

"We are only about fifty miles from the base. That's not too bad, right?"

"Well, look at you trying to be all optimistic," He said smiling down at me.

"You got a problem with that?" I asked with a sarcastic yet playful tone.

"Nope, no problem at all. Although I was thinking that if you just stood along the road and flashed those nice legs of yours maybe someone would give us a ride." He looked at me then and waggled his eyebrows.

"Ha! Never going to happen," I said as I playfully punched him in the arm. Max then quickly stole a kiss and the scruff of his unshaven face, poking my chin, made me giggle. He grabbed the baseball cap out of my hand and slapped it on my head.

"You ready?" he asked.

"Are you?" I countered.

Chapter 12

We then started the long walk through the hot New Mexico desert, to the one place we thought we might find salvation and safety. I glanced back at the Bronco, before it went out of sight and vowed that someday I would return for my father's car. It had taken us so far along on our journey and a small part of me felt like I was leaving something behind.

Norah and Carter chatted animatedly about what they each thought was going on in the world. "More like what was going wrong in the world," I mumbled under my breath.

He showed her his demon dictionary and when she expressed her agreement that the knowledge he had collected was in her words "genius", they became quick nerd buddies. Carter encouraged her to tell him everything she knew about the demon at the city hall building, any detail she knew that we didn't already have.

As I walked behind them, half listening to their conversation and half admiring Max's butt in front of me, I wondered pointlessly how Norah was able to write in Carter's book and walk at the same time. She had apparently acquired a large amount of information that Carter deemed important as well as details on other demons we had yet encountered. She spoke of how she survived when all hell broke loose, literally. Her tale was not much different than our own. When the rest of the world panicked, turning to crime, looting and worse, we chose to lay low and not let hysteria and fear take control. We watched the world around us crumble through the windows of our home and now we were walking through the rubble.

Taya was walking with Judy trying her best to comfort the younger girl. If I were to have to guess I would have said she was only a couple years younger than Taya, maybe thirteen or fourteen. The young girl, whose name we learned was Savannah, quickly warmed up to Taya. They chatted about their favorite TV shows and what teenage heart-throb they thought was the most swoon-worthy.

Judy took on the role of mother hen, making sure we took breaks regularly and drank water while also trying to conserve it. Her calm demeanor was comforting but also a little unsettling. I wasn't sure yet how I felt about her, but that may have had something to do with her crazy husband. I later told myself that I would have to look past that since she was of course going to be living with us on the base. She obviously didn't share the same insane tendencies as he did, otherwise she wouldn't have escaped with us. Or did she do that because she knew if she had stayed she would be long dead by now.

I felt someone watching me and looked up to see

Judy looking at me. I felt a bit embarrassed to think I was just having paranoid ramblings in my head about her and gave her a polite smile. She returned it and I could tell it was sincere.

I watched her for a moment longer as she wiped sweat from her brow and saw the bandage on her forearm completely exposed. She had removed her button down blouse and tied it around her waist making the full extent of the damage easy to see. Seeing that made all my doubts I had about her disappear. I didn't even want to imagine the trauma that she had to have gone through, having had her husband slash open her arm to feed her blood to some talking demon from hell.

Finding it hard to look away I walked a little quicker to catch up with Max and Carter who was even farther ahead. "You look really flushed. We should take a break."

"I'm fine Abs, we should keep going."

"We are never going to make if we all pass out from heat stroke." He gave in then and we all walked off the road to find some small bit of shade in the sparse vegetation.

Carter made rounds as we all sat panting and resting, making sure everyone was doing ok. "Everyone doing alright? We can do this. We are just walking, this ain't nothing."

"You sound like you are getting us ready for the big game, coach." Max teased.

"Hey, whatever works," I added. Carter was right, we needed to stay motivated. Just focusing on the goal, getting to the military base. We were on the home stretch now. Carter paced back and forth a moment, obviously anxious to make it to the base but also to keep his muscles warm as he had much more endurance than the rest of his. I suppose he could finally prove to Max now how useful track and field was.

I saw Taya sitting under the shade of a large bush with Savannah, both of them rubbing their feet. Their flushed faces glistened with perspiration as they continually chatted about ridiculous topics, obviously both making every effort to avoid talking about anything serious. I decided I could use a distraction as well and joined them.

The sand under the tree was cool on our feet and

was a welcome relief from the miles of walking we had done. I tried to rest while placing my head on my bag and listening to the methodic sound of the girls chatting. That, coupled with the familiar weight of my shotgun resting across my chest, let me think I might almost be able to fall asleep. Although tempting, I knew it would only be a bad idea, cause when I woke up I would only be more tired than before I went to sleep.

"Abby, may I speak with you?" Judy asked. The sound of her voice startled me a bit and I nearly jumped up.

"Yeah, sure. What's up?" I asked trying to collect myself.

She ushered me out of earshot from the girls and led me over to another large bush where Max and Carter stood waiting.

"What's going on?" I asked starting to grow concerned.

"Nothing is wrong, so don't start getting all freaked out," Carter said, sounding too much like our father. I looked at his face and noticed the sun had started to burn his nose. Coupled with the swollen eye;

he was not looking to well. Max, on the other hand, wasn't burnt at all and was turning a golden brown that I found surprisingly attractive.

"I'm not freaked out."

"I just thought we should all discuss what the plan is."

"The plan for what?" I said clearly not understanding what they were getting at. I didn't understand what more "plan" we needed than to continue walking and get to the military base.

"Abby, we aren't going to make it to the base tonight. We are walking too slowly. We would have to walk all night long to make it. It's probably going to be sunset in a couple of hours," Max said.

"Well, how much farther do you think we have to go?" I asked. It felt like we had already been walking for an eternity.

"Probably another forty miles. We are going to need to find a place to sleep for the night." The thought of having to sleep outside was definitely not something I wanted to have to do.

"Why do we have to stop? We can walk through

the night just fine, we just need to follow the road anyway right?"

"We shouldn't travel at night, it's not safe, and I don't think Savannah can handle much more," Judy said.

I saw the sincere concern in her eyes and I looked back at Savannah. Judy was right; I didn't think she could make it much longer. She was thin and frail and I could tell how much more tired she looked than everyone else, but she didn't complain. Compared to Taya, the two girls looked very similar, but Taya had a hidden strength about her that Savannah did not.

"Ok, what's the plan?" I asked.

Carter quickly pulled out a map and opened it before us. "If we walk until sunset that should give us another four hours or so and we can get about another twenty miles, so… that should put us somewhere around here." He said pointing to a location on the map.

"White sands? What's that?" I asked.

"They are sand dunes. They stretch out for quite a ways. My husband and I hiked them once about ten years ago. We should do our best to make it at least to there before we break for the night. We will have to go off the road for a bit, but that may be a better idea to be secluded than be sleeping near a bunch of abandoned vehicles or areas where demons have places to hide," Judy said.

"Neither of those sleeping arrangements sound good to me, so you guys decide," I said. Max and Carter looked at each other and then off into the distance ahead of us as if they could see the white dunes waiting for us. Neither of them wanted to say it, but from years of knowing both of them I knew what they were thinking.

"Guess we're sleeping in the dunes," I said a little annoyed and immediately stalked off. I wasn't sure if it was the fact that I had to accept we weren't going to make it to the military base until the next day, or the fact that I had to sleep outside in the dark, that was pissing me off.

We rested for about another ten minutes before we headed off again down the road. Not wanting to walk with anyone at the moment, I took the lead and walked at the head of the group. The guys knew me well enough to give me my space when I needed it without me even having to ask. A lesson they learned the hard way a long time ago.

The last few hours of light seemed to go by rather quickly, but I knew no matter how fast it felt that time was going, we were not moving any faster. The sky was holding onto the last rays of light as we neared the dunes.

We had to walk a good way off the highway to get deep enough into the dunes that we felt safe to settle in for the night. Taya was just as unhappy with the idea as I was when I told her what we were doing, maybe even more so.

"What if there are spiders or scorpions out here?" Taya asked sounding extremely whiny.

"They would be the least of our worries at the moment, don't you think?" I said. She nodded her agreement, but she looked around at the sands with a watchful eye.

Taya and I sat near a small fire the guys had built, listening to it crackle and hiss as it burned the small bushes they yanked out of the ground.

"Is she sleeping?" I asked Judy as she settled

down next to us. As hot as it was during the day the night quickly chilled around us.

"Almost as soon as she laid down. Norah is sitting with her for a while, just in case she wakes up," Judy said as she stared at the faint figure of Norah in the distance stroking Savannah's hair.

"What's wrong with her?" Taya asked in her usual manner of never thinking before she spoke.

"I don't know. I think she was sick before everything happened, but she won't talk about it," Judy said.

"Where is her family?" Taya asked.

"Gone. We found her hiding inside a police station. My guess is she was trying to find help, but the place was empty. I don't know how long she was there till we found her." Judy sighed as she accepted the bottle of water we were passing around.

I dug into my bag and pulled out my radio, setting it on the ground in front of me. "What are you doing?" Carter asked as he approached, dropping a handful of plants he just yanked out of the ground.

"I just wanted to see if I could hear it. We are so

close we should be able to pick up a signal, right?" I knew it probably looked a little desperate, but I thought the sound of that transmission would relax me.

"Leave her alone dude, if she wants to listen to it let her." Max added while dumping another pile of bushes onto the ground.

Max sat down crossing his legs and got to work on breaking down the bushes into manageable pieces. As cold as it was, I wanted to shove all the bushes straight into the fire, but I knew we couldn't let it get too large. Even though it was small, the flames burned through the small, dried twigs much too quickly. However, it emitted a strange aroma unlike any campfire I'd been around before.

Norah sat down by the fire, quietly flipping through the pages of Carter's book. The silence in the group was growing awkward and I didn't care if I was the one to break it. Everyone was trying their best to avoid the obvious, but I wanted to know what was really going on.

"How did your husband manage to lock up that demon?" I asked Judy. Everyone gave me a shocked look, but I was only asking what everyone else was too afraid to do themselves.

"I didn't witness it myself. When they attacked I took all the women and children into a room and we locked ourselves in. My son left us to help his father. We could hear the demons outside, and men's voices yelling. Then the sounds grew closer, we could tell the demons were inside the building."

Her eyes were watering then, and I could see that recounting the story was hard for her. I should have, but I didn't feel bad about making her relive it and she continued so she must have wanted to get it off her chest. My thought was that perhaps after the death of her son, they never spoke of it, as if it never happened. It was obvious that Judy did not want to pretend that her son was never there or that he did not exist.

"I could hear my son and John shouting. Bullets were flying and slamming into walls and demons alike. When the fighting was over my son came to check on us and that was when it grabbed him. It was lurking in the shadows and snatched him as he opened the door. I'll never forget the look of complete shock on his face. He managed to drive his knife into its neck before it killed him. I watched my son die and then I watched the demon turn toward us."

"Damn," Max said under his breath.

Judy swallowed hard and continued. "Jerry and Roger showed up then, they unloaded both their weapons into and it still didn't go down. I could see in their eyes they were going to leave us there. They were going to let the demon have us as they escaped, but then Norah showed up." Judy looked up at Norah, choking on her words as tears finally poured down her face.

"What happened then?" Taya asked Norah when it was clear Judy could not go on.

"I didn't want to hide when the demons attacked. I had wanted to help. I grabbed the shovel I used in the garden and shoved it into the demons midsection as hard as I could. I kept stabbing at it again and again. I knew I wasn't doing enough damage, but I was buying us time. John showed up as the demon bit into my shovel, snapping it in half. He unloaded his rifle into the demon as it lunged for us. It finally fell then, dead in its tracks and landed on the floor like a ton of bricks."

"So then you all just decided to lock it up then?" I asked.

"No, we thought it was dead. John and Judy were holding their sons body, when I noticed it was still breathing. I regret having ever said anything; I wish I would have just grabbed my broken shovel and jammed it into its neck until I took its head off." The anger in Norah's voice seemed uncharacteristic for her. She was normally very put together, even for an apocalypse, but as she described her clear disgust for the demon she wrung her hands around the hem of her shirt until her knuckles were white.

"I shouted that it was still alive and John turned toward me. The look in his eyes scared me almost as much as the demons. He quickly ordered Roger and Jerry to help him. They tied it up then and dragged it into the basement. We didn't even see John again for three days. He stayed in the basement with it all day long. I don't know what he was doing or what happened in those three days, but when he came back up he had it in his head that we had to sacrifice ourselves to the demon in order to discover its weaknesses. He wanted to know who the demon desired most, so he could use them as a pawn to get information. He wanted to avenge his son; he wanted to kill every demon on earth and was willing to do anything to do that."

"I think he was possessed," Carter said so calmly as if that were a completely normal thing to mention in a conversation. Judy turned her head toward him, clearly shocked, but she didn't say anything. "I mean it makes sense doesn't it? He was locked down there with that demon for three days. If you think about it, the thing was injured; it probably convinced John that feeding it human blood would somehow get it to reveal secrets, when really it was wanting to rebuild its strength."

"I guess we will never really know," Norah said as she rubbed the bandage on her arm where John had cut her.

"Are you ok?" I asked pointing to her arm.

She nodded then and said, "I'm going to try and get some sleep."

"I think I will too." Judy added.

Chapter 13

"Can you believe that?" Taya whispered when Judy and Norah were out of earshot. "That's horrible."

"That's not even the worst of it." Carter added as he tossed some branches into the fire.

"What do you mean?" I asked.

"Norah left out some details, probably because she didn't want to scare the two of you."

"Well what do you want to scare us for?" Taya asked.

"I'm not trying to scare you. I just think you

should know everything. When John came back up from the basement, it wasn't just human blood he wanted to sacrifice. He said it only had to be the blood of a woman, because they are considered more pure then men, and therefore would be more desired by the demon." Our jaws dropped at this comment. "Didn't you two notice that none of the men at that place had cuts on their arms?"

I shook my head not knowing what to say. Thinking back on it, I couldn't remember seeing any of the men with bandages on their arms.

"But John said that everyone had to make the sacrifice." I don't know why I said that, it sounded like I was pleading a case for John.

"Come on Abby, you really think you can believe anything that man said?" Carter asked and I shook my head.

"Now I'm really not going to get any sleep," Taya commented.

"Maybe you are right Carter. It's scary to think that we could have been that man's targets. This just throws everything into a whole new kind of crazy. All along we have been thinking that they were just savage beasts, but now they can talk and possess people?" I could feel my hope of survival slipping. I thought before that we may stand some kind of chance against them, but now I was not so sure.

"That's not entirely true." Max countered and I thought he was just trying to comfort me. "Maybe that was a higher level demon, I mean it is a lot different than the other ones we've seen. It was more... what's the word I'm looking for?"

"Aware." Carter made sounds like he was on the verge of an epiphany. "Max does have a point, as crazy as that feels to say that." Max flipped Carter the bird playfully, but Carter ignored it and went on. "When I went through my whole Goth stage after mom died, I did a lot of research on witchcraft, vampires and even demonology. They aren't all the same. This is why I have been wanting to catalog as much about them. Some of them, like the one we saw at city hall, have a more developed set of "skills", for lack of a better word, than say the birds or the little gremlin things at the camp." I tried hard not to let the fact that he mentioned our mother distract me.

She had died in a car accident when I was very little and I have no memory of her other than pictures that my father and Carter would show me. I use to be very jealous of the fact that Carter had memories of a mother I never knew, and even though I had gotten over it, I still felt a twinge of sadness whenever she was mentioned.

"So what you are saying is things could get worse than this? That there might be an even higher level demon out there?" I asked, hoping he was going to say no, but I knew he would not.

"Unfortunately. After what Norah has told me, I think things could get much worse. I'm not even sure if what we have seen are actually demons now. They could just simply be beasts or tortured souls who have been twisted into grotesque forms and let loose on the world."

"This is crazy." I almost shouted, not wanting to believe what he was saying.

"Abs calm down, it's going to be ok," Max said, resting his hand over mine.

"I can't deal with this right now. We are almost to the base. Why are we even worrying about this stuff right now? If there are worse things out there, then just let the damn military deal with it. We've done our part." Taya was starting to get heated, obviously out of fear that was getting the best of her. "I can't listen to you guys anymore, stop trying to make it worse."

"Taya we aren't trying to make it worse, I'm just being a realist and telling you what I think is going on. Do you want me to lie to you?" Carter asked.

"Yes! Things are already worse than any of us could possibly have imagined in our most horrible nightmares and you want to tell me things are going to get worse, I just can't take it!" Taya stormed off then, walking into the distance toward the top of a smaller dune. I agreed with Taya. Now really was not the time to be worrying about these things, all we should be focusing on is getting to the military base. We shouldn't be making things any harder on ourselves then they already are.

"You should probably go after her," I said looking to Carter. He was gingerly touching his swollen eye with his fingertips.

"What, why me? She's the one that's over reacting. I'm not the one who sent these demons out."

"Carter, don't you get it? She's scared, and damn it I am too. Think about everything she has gone through. We are almost to the base, just when we think we might finally be safe, you go and tell us that everything is even worse than we think it is." I shouted the words at him harsher than I had intended, but I needed to get it through his thick skull. He stood there for a moment considering what I had said.

"Besides, she shouldn't be sitting out there alone anyway." Max added.

"Max is right. At least go check on her Carter."

Without saying anything Carter nodded and headed up the small dune to stand beside Taya. I watched their forms standing in the white sand for a moment. Their bodies bathed in the light of the full moon that reflected off the white sandy dunes.

"Think she will be ok?" Max asked sounding sincerely concerned.

"Yeah, I think she has just reached her limit.

That was a pretty big bomb Carter just dropped on us. There is no way to really prepare yourself for something like that, and we are worn pretty thin already at the moment."

"How are you holding up?" Max held my face in his hands, brushing back my hair as he looked at me.

"Honestly? I'm scared out of my mind, but I feel almost numb to it all, like it won't soak in. What are we going to do Max? What are we going to do if Carter is right?"

Max pulled me into his arms and kissed my head. "Tomorrow we are going to get to that base Abby. That's what we are going to do. We are going to tell the military everything that we know and then we are going to help them fight. Everything is going to be ok."

"Do you really think so?" I asked wanting to believe what he was telling me.

"Of course I think so, and I'm never wrong am I?" He looked down at me with a smirk and I kissed him.

My emotions took over me and I took his lips against mine and kissed him more deeply than I have ever kissed anyone. I felt warm tears trickle across our lips and I could feel the pain and fear I had held onto and buried away slowly break free, if only for a moment.

Our single moment of bliss quickly shattered at the sound of Taya shrieking at the top of her lungs. Max and I jumped up to see her and Carter nearly tumbling down the dune toward us.

I started to rush for them, but Max quickly snatched my arm and pointed to the top of the dune. "Don't Abs."

"What? Why not?"

"Abby look! It's a hound."

"I don't care, that's my brother." I shouted as I yanked my arm from his grasp and ran for my shotgun. I sprinted the short distance to Carter and Taya. Just as we neared each other the sound of another hound came from my left.

A second hound was descending upon us. Judy noticed it quickly and was scrambling to shake Norah and Savannah awake.

"They are surrounding us!" Max shouted as he ran up behind me.

"Get over here!" I yelled for Judy and the others to come toward us, but they were moving too slowly in their fear as they kept stumbling in the thick sand. My heart pounded in my chest as I tried to figure out what we should do.

The hounds slowly made their way down the dune, closing in on us. Carter grabbed his crossbow and quickly landed an arrow into the head of the first hound. It wailed in pain and swiped at the arrow with its paw, but it didn't stop in its descent.

They continued steadily moving in on us. Taya quickly pulled out my knife from the strap on my leg and held it in front of her, while Max handed a smaller knife to Norah. We joined together, our bodies trembling as we prepared for the assault.

Carter fired another arrow at the second demon. It hit with a heavy thud into its shoulder. They were about twenty feet from us now, stepping back and forth. Then I realized that the demon hounds had done something we had never seen them do before, they stood and watched us. Their black fur glistened in the moonlight displaying the ripples of muscle under their large bodies.

"They aren't attacking. Why aren't they attacking?" I asked as the breeze carried their rotting stench into my nostrils. I gagged, but didn't dare try to cover my nose because I needed both my hands free.

Savannah screamed from inside Judy's arms and she pointed toward the dune behind us. We all turned quickly and saw, at the top of the dune was the demon from the basement of city hall.

It looked like a massive bear atop the dune. It stood up onto its hind legs and howled into the night. Its growl was unlike any animal I had ever heard. We pulled in closer to each other as the demon glared down at us.

"Dear God," Judy said, her voice shaking in fear. I could feel everyone beginning to panic as it walked slowly toward us.

"It followed us!" Taya yelled in panic.

The demon turned its head toward the second hound and suddenly it bolted into a sprint toward us to attack. Carter and I jumped into action as it came barreling toward us with its teeth barred. Carter fired another arrow at it as it opened its mouth in a loud snarl. I watched the arrow fly into the back of its mouth and I pulled the trigger of my shotgun hitting it right in the head sending its body falling into the sand at our feet.

    I glanced at the dead hound for a moment, just long enough to ensure it was dead. I heard a gun fire and quickly turned to see Max fighting the first hound. He already unloaded his clip and was holding his knife at the ready. Taya was shaking, barely holding onto her knife as her body trembled in fear. I shoved her aside with my shoulder as I ran to Max's side and cocked my shotgun. I blasted the demon and only slowed it, but Max lunged quickly. Slicing the demons throat as blood sprayed onto us.

    Dark blood gushed in streaks across my jeans and I swallowed the urge to vomit at the foul stench coupled with the scent of blood. I glanced over at Judy and Norah who were holding Savannah tightly between them. Their eyes were full of fear as they stood like deer caught in headlights.

    As the second demon hound fell the large demon from city hall leaped for us like a lion. We all ran, but

Savannah was frozen in fear. Judy remained tugging at her arm, but couldn't get her to move fast enough, finding it difficult to get traction in the sand.

Carter grabbed his last arrow, knocked it and I watched him take a deep breath as he tried to steady his shot as the demon fell onto Savannah. Max ran for it, slicing off an ear, but it fiercely swatted him with his paw like he was a fly, sending him soaring in the air to land like a rock ten feet away.

Carter took his shot and the arrow sliced right through the demon's eye. It roared in pain as blood streaked down its face and dripped off its muzzle. Judy screamed as she tried to drag Savannah's body away. The little girl's form looked like a bloody rag doll as Judy pulled her across the sand. Taya quickly ran to help, tears streaming down her face and I knew this was our only chance.

I fumbled trying to reload my shotgun and only managed to load one shot before the demon started for Carter and me. He pulled out his knife as I fired the shotgun into the demon's face. Blood splattered everywhere as the shots hit it, but it only shook its head violently before continuing its advance. I went to pull my knife, but realized Taya had taken it earlier.

Suddenly Max came flying at the demon, he slammed his knife into the demon's back and held on as it swung and bucked trying to get him off. I was relieved to see he was ok, but the sight of Max's body flinging around like that made me sick to my stomach. Carter looked to me and then at the demon, slicing at its face and trying to dodge its swings. "Load your gun!" Carter shouted.

I bolted into action and dove for the bullets I had dropped on the ground. I quickly loaded them and realized I couldn't get a shot. If I fired I would hit Max who was still being violently tossed like a cowboy riding a bucking bull.

Max saw my struggling and quickly released as the demon bucked, sending him flying again across the dark landscape.

"Move!" I shouted at Carter. He jumped out of the way but not before the demon thrashed at him, hitting his legs and sending him tumbling face down into the sand. I pulled the trigger and the spray of bullets flew into the demons face.

It howled so loudly I wanted to cover my ears and then it looked right at me. Our eyes locked and I had never been so terrified in my life, as its eyes bore into me. Into my soul. I could feel my body freezing in fear, but I couldn't turn my eyes from it. A sense of overwhelming dread crept through my body like thousands of tiny spiders crawling under my skin. My mind filled with images of horrifying sights that I had never witnessed before and my body trembled as the demon dug at the ground like it was readying itself to charge at me. My breathing grew quick and ragged as my body trembled in fear.

I squeezed my eyes shut as he came for me, tensing my body for the pain I knew was coming, but it never did. I opened my eyes to see that Judy had thrown herself in front of me.

The demon had latched onto her and was shaking her around like a dog would a chew toy. She had to have been in tremendous pain, but she was screaming out in pure rage as the demon clamped down on her midsection. She repeatedly stabbed at it with a knife until it bit down even harder, severing her in half.

The sight of Judy's body falling to the ground in pieces made me drop to my knees. Complete defeat washed through me and I lost all hope. All I could manage was to repeat in my head over and over that we were all going to die.

Suddenly, Norah was at my side trying to load my shotgun as I sat frozen in shock, watching the demon devour Judy into two quick bites.

"Abby!" Norah screamed at me and hit me hard in the face and I felt blood trickle from my nose. My face burned, but it broke me from whatever trance the demon had placed on me.

Just as she handed me the shotgun the demon slashed at her with its claws, her blood splattering all over my face. I saw the whites of her eyes expand as she looked at me in agonizing fear and pain. She gurgled and blood began to pour from her mouth as her body fell onto me. I screamed out in rage as the weight of Norah's body collapsed on me.

I quickly caught her and dropped her to the ground, trying to avoid the demon as it swung at me. I desperately tried to get back on my feet as I struggled to get away, but the demon was gaining on me. I scrambled through the sand trying to gain my footing as the demon took its time as if it were enjoying itself immensely.

I saw something move from the corner of my eye and saw Carter running at full speed toward the demon. Then I saw Max coming from the other direction, both of them screaming a battle cry as they carried their knives above them. They each lunged for the demons neck, slicing as deeply as they could. As their blades tore through the soft flesh of its neck I felt arms grab me.

Taya dragged me farther away as I watched the demon stagger. It whipped around and slammed Carter to the ground. It quickly smashed its large claw onto Carter. He struggled and grunted as it pressed down on his chest with its giant paw.

Max lifted his knife again and sent it screaming down the demons neck. The demon staggered again and looked up at Max, its body shuddering. It tried to bite at Max while keeping Carter contained under its foot. Fear for Max and Carter coursed through me as I saw them struggling in their fight.

I quickly wiggled out of Taya's grip on me and pried the gun out of Norah lifeless hand. "Get Carter!" I shouted to Taya as I ran for the demon. She followed close at my heels and quickly grabbed Carter's arms trying to pull him out from under the demon's foot. The demon's eyes were on me and he ignored Taya as she struggled futilely to free Carter.

I ran to Max's side as I loaded my last two rounds and cocked the shotgun. Max saw me and dove to the side to avoid being bitten. Just as the demon turned his head I fired at the open wound in its neck, quickly firing again, before the demon turned for me. It tried to move, but faltered. Blood was gushing from its neck into dark pools on the white sand. As the demon began to slip and struggle for footing in its puddles of blood Max took another final swing, completely severing the demons head.

It fell to the ground and rolled to my feet, leaving its black eyes looking up at me.

"Abby, Abby are you ok?" Max ran to me, squeezing me close to him. We both began to weep as we shuddered in each other's arms.

"I'm ok I think. Are you hurt?" I asked and he shook his head.

Not wanting to feel the demons eyes on me I ran to where Carter lay on the ground. "Oh my God, is he ok?" I asked Taya as I ran to my brother's side.

"I'm ok Abby." I hugged him as tightly as I could without hurting him and he let out a slight grunt, but didn't tell me to let go.

"Is it dead?" Taya asked, her voice wavering.

"Yeah, it's dead," Max said with satisfaction.

"What should we do now?" I asked as I helped Carter get up.

"Well, we definitely can't stay here can we?" Carter said, anger building in his tone.

I saw Taya staring at the bodies that lay strewn about our tiny campfire. I grabbed her shoulder and tried to turn her head away. "Don't look at them Taya. Don't remember them like this."

"Why not? You want me to just forget them then?"

"That's not what I meant," I stammered. The

anger in her voice surprised me.

"Of course that's what you meant! You only care about yourself, it's your fault they're dead. You just stood there like an idiot!" Taya got in my face then as she continued to blame me.

"Hey! Calm down!" Max shouted as he pushed Taya away from me.

"Stay out of this; you just want to protect your little girlfriend!" Taya countered shoving Max back.

"Huh, what?" Carter said clearly still trying to gain his senses.

"Listen to what you're saying Taya, do you really believe Abby is to blame for all of this?" Max asked. I stood there, starting to wonder if she was right. I was starting to question myself, what was I doing just standing there? It really was my fault that Judy and Norah were dead.

"She just stood there Max, you saw her! Why did you do it? Why Abby?" Taya was sobbing almost uncontrollably, as tears and snot ran down her face. Everyone looked to me; they too wanted to know what had come over me.

"I... I don't know. When it looked me in the eyes, I couldn't move. It was like I could feel it inside me. Inside my head, under my skin. I just couldn't move Taya. I didn't mean to... I didn't want this to happen." I pictured in my mind what I must have looked like to them, just watching the demon attacking everyone, just watching it killing Norah and I started to feel sick to my stomach.

"It's ok," Max whispered to me as he put his arm around me to steady me on my feet. Taya's blood boiled at the sight of Max comforting me and she slapped me hard in the face before storming off. I stood there in shock and pain as my face burned from the strike. She had hit me right were Norah had, right before she died. I wiped the blood from my nose and watched Taya in the distance as she started to pack up what she could, being careful to stay far away from the demon bodies.

"She didn't mean that. She's just upset," Carter said trying to comfort me. "I need you to stay focused Abby. I need you to tell me what happened to you."

"Not now Carter." I protested shoving his hand away from me.

"Fine, but we need to know. If they are able to control people like that then we need to know how to stop it. I guess that adds some weight to the idea that John was possessed by it."

That made me start to panic. "You think I'm possessed?"

"No, I just think it saw you as a threat and was able to make contact with you somehow and immobilized you while it focused on…other targets." He paused trying to find the right words. "I need my tough girl back. Can you do that for me?"

"You sound like Dad," I said.

"Yeah, well, it always seemed to work for him, when he said it."

I thought about it for a moment and nodded my head at him. As much as I wanted to crawl into a ball and cry the rest of the night I buried my emotions, and sucked it up like I always had to. I always had to be Daddy's tough little girl.

I watched Carter walk over to Taya and was grateful that he was playing diplomat. I wanted so badly for everything to be over, for us to just get to the military base and then everything would be better.

"You don't always have to be tough, ya know?" Max said softly to me.

"Yes I do. If I let myself feel everything, I don't know if I could handle it."

"You don't need to handle it Abs, I'm here. Carter and Taya are here too, although Taya not so much right now, but that will pass. What I'm trying to say is it's ok to freak out. I can see you holding it all back. I know you are trying to be strong for everyone. We are still going to love you even if you flip out and throw a tantrum like Taya, just like you'll still love her even though she's a teenage emotional rollercoaster." He smiled at me and tried to clean up my face with a strip of his shirt he had torn off.

"She has good reason to though." I winced as he put pressure on my nose.

He shrugged. "Maybe so. Everyone has reason to freak out right now, the world has turned into the devil's playground, but she didn't need to take it out on you. Now, take a deep breath and then I need you to help me get things packed up."

"Ok Dr. Phil," I said using humor to lighten the mood like Max always did.

"There's my girl!" a wide grin spreading on his face. His optimism drove me nuts, but I couldn't survive without it. I watched him as he made his way toward our things and noticed that he was limping slightly. I realized he must have been in pain from the fight with the demons and I wanted so badly for him to never feel pain again. I silently prayed, not caring that God had apparently forsaken us, that we would all make it to the base and that someday we would be able to live the lives that we had always wanted to.

"I love you Max." I called out to him.

"I love you too." He shouted back at me. I took a deep breath and walked to what was left of our camp.

We spent the next hour or two packing up anything we had left that was still usable. Max and Carter stacked the demons bodies in a large pile and used what was left of the tiny bit of gasoline we had to set them on fire. Strangely enough they lit easily and burned like dry wood. The fire grew large and we all felt uncomfortable being near such a large beacon of light, not to mention the stench.

We had wanted to bury Savannah and Norah but we didn't have any tools, nor did we have the time to do it by hand. We pulled them as far away from the demons as we could and had a small funeral, each of us saying our own prayers silently. I could feel Taya's eyes on me the whole time.

It was difficult to just leave them lying there, and the thought of animals or other demons getting to them was difficult to bear. Carter suggested that we set them ablaze as well, and after Taya's protests he convinced her that in many cultures it was a very respectful way to honor the dead.

As the orange glow of the flames danced across our tear stained faces we turned our back on our lost friends and made our way back toward the highway.

It felt like an eternity of walking before the slightest rays of sunlight blossomed on the horizon. None of us said much on the long walk, except when one of us needed a break. We didn't stray from the road and wouldn't even allow ourselves much privacy to go to the bathroom. The farther down the road we got, the slower we became. Our bodies were weakening from the lack of sleep and food.

I'll never forget the moment we saw the military

base in the distance. A sudden wash of relief spilled over me and I felt like I could breathe again. We cheered and hugged each other and our steps felt lighter as we quickened our advance to the base.

"I'm going to take the longest shower ever," Taya said sounding much more like herself then she had earlier that night.

"Me too, but not before I stuff my face with whatever they have to eat." Max added.

I smiled over at Carter and I could visibly tell how relieved he looked, even with his face battered up. We had made it.

"How are we going to get in when we get there?" I asked as I wondered if they had some kind of perimeter set up.

"Duh! Right through the front gate," Taya said sounding like walking into a military base during a demon apocalypse was completely normal.

"Taya's right. We probably should head for the front gate, I'm sure they have some kind of surveillance set up. When they see us approaching they will probably send someone to meet us."

"I can't wait." Not holding back my relief I sped up my walking as much as my feet would allow. Max slowed down to keep pace with me and I mouthed the words *I love you* to him and he smiled.

The closer and closer we got the more relieved I felt. As we neared the front of the base we walked quickly down the freeway ramp and onto First Street. The visitor parking area was loaded with cars of every kind and we looked at each other with tearful grins from ear to ear.

"So many people have come," I said. "Do you think we should wait here for them to send someone to get us?"

"Heck no!" Carter said, a laugh almost escaping him.

"What if they have like, shooters guarding the entrance?" Taya said starting to sound paranoid as she looked up at a tall watch tower.

"I'm sure they do, but they aren't going to shoot humans," Max said reassuring her. "We've made it this far, don't get hesitant now."

I wanted to say something to comfort her as well,

but she was still angry at me. I could tell she was trying to work past it and wasn't glaring at me as much, but it was obvious she was still hurt. Whether she was right or wrong didn't matter, so I didn't want to press my luck.

As we made our way further into the base down the main road, I kept waiting for a military jeep to come rolling up to us, but nothing ever happened. I knew it was crazy to expect the entire base would be jam packed full of people, and operating busily like it normally would have, but I guess I secretly did hope that.

We slowed our pace and it was obvious that we all were starting to worry. We walked further and further into the base and no one stopped us.

"Where is everyone?" Taya asked.

"I'm sure they have everyone concentrated in one area. This base is pretty spread out; they would want to be able to keep an eye on everyone," Carter said.

"Well, where is the concentrated area then?" Taya snapped.

"The radio tower?" I questioned. "I mean they use it for transmissions, so they would be nearby there right?"

"Good point, Abs!" Max smiled at me.

We each looked around trying to find some kind of radio tower or satellite dish on any of the buildings.

"Over there!" Taya shouted as she jumped excitedly and pointed off to our left. We all squinted into the distance and could barely make out the sight of a large object turning around and around.

"That's it! Come on!" Carter took off at a steady trot and we all followed at his heels. As we ran, I wondered what it would be like to finally see the military. Throughout history the military had always stood as a beacon of hope, protection, freedom and defense. I imagined formidable looking men dressed in military uniforms carrying massive guns. The thought brought a smile to my face as I ran.

We all skidded to a halt when we made it to the radio tower. We glanced around us waiting for someone to show up. The satellite spun steadily as it towered above us and as the silence of the base came crashing down on me, I could feel fear threatening to break me.

"There's no one here. What are we going to do?" Taya was panicked.

"They're here. Don't say that," Carter demanded.

"Let's find the door to this place," Max said rushing around the side of the building. I followed him in silence, not wanting to admit to myself what I was slowly starting to realize, there was no one here.

Carter tried every knob in a panicked state. It would crush him if he was wrong. We had finally made it to the base, we had risked our lives to make it here and it could have been all for nothing.

Max found an open door and we all rushed eagerly inside to an empty hallway. There were papers and boxes lining the walls, but the disorder and clutter was a normal site. Papers crunched under our feet as we walked slowly down the halls. I squeezed Max's hand for comfort as we all walked single file behind Carter.

Some of the walls were smeared with blood that had dried a long time ago, leaving dark streaks. That was not what really scared me. The claw marks that tore through the plaster confirmed my worst fears. The demons had made it here. I didn't want to admit it aloud and I desperately tried to focus my thoughts elsewhere as we continued through the halls.

We glanced into rooms, randomly making our way to whatever room was the control room for the satellite. There had to be someone there controlling it, I thought to myself. We needed someone to be there. I tried to convince myself that we would find someone. Maybe he fell asleep on duty, or maybe they set it on autopilot. Those things run on autopilot right?

"Maybe everyone is still sleeping?" I said. It was a ridiculous comment but I just couldn't let myself believe that we had come this far only to find the base empty. "It's still pretty early isn't it?"

"Yeah," Carter said not sounding convinced. I knew it was a silly thought. They wouldn't all be sleeping, someone would be standing guard.

As we turned a corner, at the end of the hallway I could see a door that was clearly labeled as the control. At the sight of it, Carter ran down the hallway vaulting for the door opening as he nearly burst into the room. It seemed as if the rest of us took a deep breath before we followed after him.

The room was lined with numerous workstations

lit up with tiny blinking lights and odd looking keypads. The foreign electronic equipment wasn't what confused me most; it was the fact that the room was completely empty and looked like it had been for quite some time.

We each walked through the room silently surveying it. As if we had to look at every inch of it before we would believe that we were truly wrong about coming here.

I took a seat at one of the computers and wiped the dust off the screen. I couldn't make sense of any of the information I was seeing and looked up to see what Carter was doing.

He was standing at what looked like the main workstation; both his hands were twisted through his hair. Max was nearby noisily rummaging through papers. He must have sensed something and he caught me staring at him. I quickly tried to mask the fear on my face, but he knew me too well for that to work.

"Maybe they had to move? There has to be something here. They wouldn't keep the transmission running if no one is here."

"It's not still running!" Carter snapped. "Just

look. It's been shut off. What we heard must have just been the signaling bouncing off of something, or maybe someone else was broadcasting it. That's probably why it's been so weak. Someone shut it off, which means they didn't want people to keep coming here." Carter started thrashing around in anger, kicking a chair over and sweeping all the papers off the workstation as he kicked the desk and sat down heavily in defeat.

"You don't know that," Taya said rushing to his side. She tried putting her arms around him but he pushed her away. Her face took on a hurt expression, but she quickly removed it and placed a hand on his arm, which he allowed.

I frantically tried to understand what was going on. I didn't know anything about computers or transmitters, but I wanted to do something, to say something but I didn't know what.

"Yeah man, we don't know that for sure yet. Maybe they shut it off cause they needed to conserve power. We can't just give up when we've come this far."

Carter just sat there, his head in his hands,

shaking. "There is no one here."

Seeing my brother so defeated brought tears to my eyes. We had come all this way and been through so much and it was all for nothing. I walked over to Carter and sat on the floor across from him.

Taya looked up at me her eyes clearly pleading me to say something, but I couldn't. Hot tears ran down my face as all the terrors of our journey fell onto me in giant waves.

"We came all this way for nothing. I'm sorry you guys, I'm so sorry. It is all my fault." Carter sounded so full of anger at himself it almost scared me.

"It wasn't all for nothing. I wouldn't be here if it weren't for you." Taya pleaded. She smiled when he looked at her, but he didn't return it.

"She's right Carter. We saved her and that definitely counts and you didn't make us come. We decided as a group we were going to do this, so don't take it all onto yourself," I said.

We weren't getting through to him and I could see his grief building as he continually shook his head and cursed himself under his breath.

I couldn't let us fall apart; we needed each other now more than ever or maybe I just needed them. I looked over to Max and he was busily flipping switches and turning knobs, trying to find anything that would be of help to us. I knew he was desperate to find something not wanting to accept that Carter was right.

"What are we going to do?" Taya asked me.

"What's wrong with you guys? Don't you get it? There…is…no…one… here!" Carter shouted at us. He quickly stood up and stormed out of the room and slammed the door in his wake sending picture frames crashing to the floor. Taya sat frozen for a moment and then ran after him.

I couldn't help myself and buried my face in my hands. I cried like a baby, not caring how I looked and holding none of it back. I didn't want to bury my fears any longer and finally let myself be weak and vulnerable.

Max was quickly at my side trying to pull my hands away from my face.

"There's no one here." I wailed through my sobs.

"You're wrong Abs, your wrong. Look at me." I reluctantly let him pull my hands away and looked into his chocolaty brown eyes. "There *are* people here Abs." He said as a small but reassuring smile spread across his lips.

"What? Where? How do you know? We need to tell Carter." My heart pounded in my chest and I couldn't believe he didn't say anything sooner. I looked at him expectantly, wiping the tears from my face.

Max brushed wet strands of hair away from my face and smiled at me again. "We're here Abby. We're here."

My body shuddered as I realized the truth in his words. I took a deep breath and squeezed his hand as I brought it to my lips. "I love you Max."

"I love you too," He said as he kissed my forehead. Then he stood up and without a hint of hesitation he turned the transmission back on.

I stood up and walked to his side, letting him take me under his arm. I stared at the orange blinking light that showed the transmission was on and watched the monitor that displayed the familiar text of the message we had all prayed would lead us to salvation.

"Do you think people will come?" I asked him.

"I hope so."

Other Titles by Megan Duncan:

Warm Delicacy Series

Savor (Book #1 coming Summer 2011)

Indulge (Book #2 coming Fall 2011)

Made in the USA
Charleston, SC
21 July 2011